MILLIE MAVEN
AND THE BRONZE MEDALLION

TED DEKKER & RACHELLE DEKKER

Cover art and design by Manuel Preitano

Printed in the U.S.A.

ISBN 978-1-7335718-3-8

$\mathcal{P}$ROLOGUE

I sometimes wonder who I might be if I'd had parents, real parents, who loved me. A mother and father who raised me in a nice, warm home with a yard and a dog. You know, a normal life.

But I didn't. No loving home, no dogs, no friends. That wasn't my path. My journey was something else entirely. Sometimes I wonder if what happened to me was even real. I'm not sure you'll believe the story I'm going to tell you. Some of you might even think I'm crazy. Either way, I can assure you that what happened changed my life forever.

My name is Millie Maven, and this is my story. Sit down and buckle up, because it's going to be a wild ride.

CHAPTER ONE

Birthdays are supposed to be special. Mine never were, but that year it was going to be different. Mother had promised me. I'd spent a week caught up in imagining what a real birthday would be like. Would there be cake? Balloons? Party guests? Surely there wouldn't be party guests. Mother never let outsiders into the house.

Earlier that month when our refrigerator died Mother insisted the local appliance store leave the new unit outside the tall iron gate. Mother had our groundskeeper and maintenance man, Roger, cart the new refrigerator up to the house and install it. Roger was an old Salvadorian man who lived in a small cottage on the property, but he wasn't really that handy. And he didn't speak English very well, much less read it.

It took him an entire afternoon to get the refrigerator working, and Mother was furious. I felt terrible for Roger, listening to Mother batter him at the top of her lungs, and I kept my distance as much as I could. I knew to steer clear when she got that way. If I'm being honest, I tried to stay out of her sight most of the time, afraid I'd do something that would transform her from Mother to Monster.

The morning of my birthday I shook away my thoughts and pushed myself off the bathroom floor, done scrubbing the white tile until it sparkled. The room smelled like lemons. I placed the brush into the bucket filled with dirty water, careful not to splash anything onto the clean floor.

I wondered if my body would ever not ache from the labor, and if hands were meant to endure so much abuse. The bathroom was one of eight in the large stone mansion that Mother's husband, Augustus Pruitt, had inherited from his wealthy grandfather, Mortimer Pruitt. Augustus was my uncle, not my father.

Mother wasn't my biological mom either, but the aunt who took me in after my real parents died in a car accident when I was a baby. She often reminded me how she'd saved me from a life of abandonment. She taught me to read and write, then left the rest of my schooling to me. She let Martha bring me books from the library. She loved me in her own way, I suppose.

Mr. Pruitt, on the other hand, hated me. One of Mother's many rules was that I must be invisible whenever Mr. Pruitt was home. He often traveled for work—something about managing international properties—but when he was in the house, I was never to let him see or hear me.

I caught a glimpse of myself in the round bathroom mirror. Skinny and pale, plain brown eyes with no sparkle, dirty-blond hair. My threadbare dress, once white, was yellowed from stains. It covered me up to my collarbone and dropped past my knees. I'd rolled the long sleeves up to my elbows, but they still got wet from my work. Maybe Mr. Pruitt would feel differently about seeing me if I didn't look like such a tramp.

"Millie?"

I turned quickly and saw Mother standing in the doorframe. She was plump and short, with poorly dyed graying hair and a round face covered by too much makeup.

"What are you doing?" Mother asked.

Her tone suggested there was a right answer, and I wasn't sure what it was.

"Have you finished all your chores already?" she asked.

"No, Mother," I answered.

"And do you think standing around daydreaming when you have so much work to do is a good use of your time?"

I dropped my eyes to the floor, ashamed. "No, Mother. I'm sorry."

She let out an annoyed huff. She walked inside and I watched as she bent over, ran her finger under the sink, then stood to examine it closely in the light. I swallowed, waiting for her verdict. She dropped her hand and I could feel her cold stare.

"Do you know what today is?" she asked.

"My birthday."

"And you know how badly I want to celebrate you. Twelve is a big year, and I've been looking forward to this evening's celebration."

I dared to look up at her. Her eyes were small and dark inside her chubby face, her signature purple eyeshadow painted on thick and messy.

"But birthday celebrations must be earned. Do you deserve a birthday, Millie?" She thrust her finger into my face. "Do you think this is worth celebrating?"

A hint of dust might have been on her finger, but I knew better than to question her. I shook my head, the only safe response.

"There will be no birthday celebration until it is earned," Mother said. "Is that understood?"

I swallowed hard against the dread rising through my chest and nodded.

She shook her head. Placing her hand under my chin, she lifted it so our eyes met, then studied me for a moment.

"You're as plain looking as my little sister was," Mother said. "Sometimes when I catch sight of you in the hall, I'm transported back to when she and I were girls. She had the same lazy, disobedient streak I see in you."

Mother didn't speak about my real mom often, but when she did it was never complimentary.

"Maybe what happened to her and your father wasn't so terrible," she continued. "At least now you have me. I hope you realize how fortunate you are, child." Mother released my chin and stepped away. "Clean it again from top to bottom. I don't want a speck of dirt anywhere."

She paused before leaving.

"Do you love me, Millie?"

I nodded.

"I want you to say it," Mother said.

"I love you, Mother." I forced a smile but my fingers were trembling.

With a shallow nod, she left me to prove my love.

✦

Morning became afternoon and I was hungry but afraid to stop and eat. If Mother saw me munching in the kitchen, she'd take my birthday celebration away for sure. I checked and rechecked surfaces, scrubbing floors and furniture until my knuckles were raw. All I could think about was cake. It had been a long time since I'd had anything sweet.

I knew the old mansion well. Three floors with an attic and ten rooms, most of which were never used. Three sitting rooms with ugly furniture and ornate decorations that Mr. Pruitt collected on his travels. Seven bedrooms with dark wooden bed frames, heavy dressers, and thick curtains, always drawn even though there were no prying eyes on five acres so far from town.

The Colorado mountain property sat in a clearing that could only be accessed by a single paved driveway. The closest town, Paradise, was nearly ten miles away, and Mother only went there when absolutely necessary. I had never been.

The acreage was mostly covered in manicured lawn accented by a small pond and tall, beautiful aspen trees. The backyard was flat and simple. Bushes ran along the rear of the house and a stone path stretched from the door to a detached garage.

The mansion also had a large library with an attached office, a rarely used dining room fitted with a long table that easily sat twelve, and a big kitchen tucked at the back of the first floor. You could usually find Martha and her nineteen-year-old daughter, Abby, working there. They took care of all the cooking and shopping and had been with the Pruitts since long before I came. They helped me with the housework on occasion.

Mother didn't like us to waste time chatting, so she forbade me from interacting with them unless I needed to. Martha was a small old woman with gray hair who hardly ever looked at me. But Abby was kind, with sweet green eyes and soft blond hair. Sometimes when she was certain Mother wasn't around, she'd wink at me or make a funny face. Her mother would scold her, but she did it anyway.

At times Abby would remain for days in the small suite behind the kitchen where she and her mother lived. Abby was sick, and I didn't know the details, but from the pain in her mother's face I believed it wasn't good. I wasn't certain, but I liked to imagine Abby was my friend and I felt sorry for her.

Martha was as scared of Mother as I was, but Abby didn't seem to share our fear. I envied her sometimes. Not just because she seemed fearless, but also because of the way Martha would smile at her when they didn't think I was watching. Martha and Abby acted differently than Mother and I did. I couldn't help but wish I had a mother who was kind to me that way.

When I finished the main floor I wiped the sweat from my brow and headed for the large supply closet at the end of the hall to get what I needed for the second floor. Inside the closet, I refilled my bucket from the utility sink, grabbed another brush, and took the broom with me so I wouldn't have to come back down for it.

Balancing it all was tricky, but I tucked the broom handle under my arm and held the bucket and brush in either hand, then headed toward the stairs that rose from the mansion's large marbled lobby.

Normally I would use the back staircase reserved for servants, but it was narrow and I wouldn't make it through with all I was carrying. And the front stairs were much faster, and I couldn't waste any time.

The main stairs were accented with two tall pillars and a massive chandelier. To the right was a sitting room with ugly pink couches and matching curtains that always smelled like dust. To the left, the library was filled with aging books, a massive oak desk, and chairs covered in yellow flowery fabric. Everything was in shadow thanks to the always drawn curtains. At least it was clean, thanks to me.

I was four steps up when I heard the voice that sent a shiver through my bones. I turned my head slowly and saw Mr. Pruitt stand from one of the library chairs, phone pressed to his ear.

He was home! Mother always told me when he would be home so I knew to keep clear of him, but she'd said nothing. If I had known I wouldn't have dared to use the front stairs. Mother would be furious if she knew. His back was to me. *Maybe if I hurry*, I thought, *I could make it up and out of sight before he sees me.*

Heart racing, I moved quickly. I was three steps from the top before I dared a glance back to make sure Mr. Pruitt hadn't spotted me. That was a mistake. The toe of my worn tennis shoe clipped the edge of the next step. Water splashed from the bucket as I tried to recover my balance. I overcorrected and nearly toppled to the side. The broom under my arm slipped free and crashed down the stairs.

Fear gripped my chest. The bang had been loud. Too loud!

I carefully placed the bucket down and tiptoed to retrieve the broom, not daring to look toward the library.

"I'll call you back," Mr. Pruitt snapped. My pulse surged.

I grabbed the broom and straightened to see Mr. Pruitt's dark stare at the bottom of the steps. He was tall and thin with pale wrinkled skin and a large pointed nose that jutted out below squinty eyes. I wasn't sure if I should move. I dared not do anything that would add to the trouble I was already in.

"Priscilla!" Mr. Pruitt thundered.

A door shut somewhere, followed by the clicking of heels against the wooden floor, and then Mother was in the hall, staring up at me. Her face darkened, and she hurried to her husband's side.

"I'm so sorry, darling, I—"

"What part of 'I never want to see or hear from this child' was not understood?" Mr. Pruitt interrupted.

"Forgive me, I—"

"I allow her to live under my roof and eat my food, and all I ask is that she obey the rules. She's an ungrateful, disobedient, worthless burden!"

Not wanting her to pay the price for my mistake, I dared speak. "I'm sorry, it was my fault."

"Do not speak to me!" Mr. Pruitt roared. He faced Mother. "If you can't keep her in line, then mark my words, I will send her to an institution where she belongs." He stormed away.

My hands trembled at my sides. Before Mother could speak, the massive front door opened. Martha and her daughter walked in with bundles of firewood in hand. They stopped at the sight of us, looking at me with pity.

"Don't you dare look at her!" Mother snapped. "She doesn't deserve your concern or attention. Until she can learn to behave, no one is allowed to look at her. Is that understood?!"

Martha dipped her head. She and Abby rushed across the entryway and out of sight. Tears stung my eyes and I did my best to hide them. They would only infuriate Mother more. *Crying makes you ugly,* Mother would say.

"How could you?" Mother demanded, glaring up at me again.

"I didn't know—"

"Don't make excuses!" she huffed. "I'm doing my best, Millie. Doing everything I can to mold you into someone worth something. But you seem intent on doing the opposite. I don't know how much more of your disappointment I can take!"

"I'm sorry, Mother."

"Do you know how hard you make it to love you?" she snapped. "Maybe Augustus is right. Maybe you're just an ungrateful, worthless burden. You should be ashamed of yourself."

A tear slipped down my cheek, but I couldn't wipe it away without being obvious.

"Go to your room until you're told otherwise." Then she left me alone on the stairs with tears snaking down my face.

CHAPTER TWO

The sound of knocking on the floor stirred me from my bed. I slept on a thin mattress in the attic, the only place Mr. Pruitt allowed me to call mine. I sat up, feeling the hard floor as I shifted, and blinked in the darkness. I flicked on the lamp. My sheet fell away and I shivered. The green digital clock Mother had given me blinked the time: 7:00 p.m.

The pounding from below came again, a broom handle hitting the trapdoor that led to my attic. It was how Mother summoned me. I stood up and moved to the small square platform in the floor that unfolded into a ladder.

The attic was large, but I kept to one corner. I had only one lamp and no windows. Even with the lamp lit, half the attic remained in shadows—a good thing because I often heard the pattering of creatures and was glad I couldn't see them.

My belongings were few and humble. A suitcase stored everything I owned—three outfits, two pairs of shoes, some old books, and some drawing materials.

I loved to draw. Once Mother let it slip that my birth mom drew as well. I liked to think I inherited the skill from her, though Mother said I wasn't very good at it. She was probably right, but I did it anyway. I taped my drawings to the wall beside my bed and stared at them when I couldn't sleep. Mostly they were sketches of places I'd dreamed up or of people that I imagined were my friends.

I pushed the hatch open and saw Martha standing below, broom in hand.

"Mrs. Pruitt would like to see you in the dining room," she said. Her sad eyes lingered on me for a prolonged beat before she turned and left.

I climbed down the ladder and headed for the stairs that descended to the first floor. I could smell something sweet wafting from the kitchen. Martha had been baking and the aroma of cake filled the cold home with warmth.

Cake! Had Mother decided to let me have a cake for my birthday after all? That could only mean that she'd forgiven me! I quickened my pace. Maybe everything was going to be okay.

I was careful to check for Mr. Pruitt as I came to the first floor. Seeing no sign of him, I headed for the large dining room next to the kitchen. The massive stone fireplace was alive with flames when I entered, and Mother was facing it, sitting in one of the red velvet chairs that surrounded the long table. On the table was a single white cupcake topped with a beautiful blue icing flower. Beside it sat a square package wrapped in birthday paper.

My heart jumped as Mother turned to me. "Hello, darling."

"Hello, Mother." I stopped a few feet from her. The warmth of the fire matched the warmth growing in my chest. It was all going to be okay. More than okay. I was now twelve years old, a young lady, and Mother did love me.

Mother gave me a thin smile. "Millie, you know that everything I do for you I do because I care about you."

I nodded. "Yes, Mother."

"I want you to be better than the stock you come from."

I nodded again, trying to be patient.

"And the only way for me to do that is to destroy

the ungrateful, disobedient nature in you. Something is wrong with you, Millie."

Her words landed like a punch to my gut.

Mother sighed. "It isn't all your fault. You were born this way. I'm the only one who loves you enough to break the bad in you."

Mother stood and plucked the wrapped gift off the table. "I was so looking forward to giving this to you. A new drawing pad and pencils." She shook her head and tossed the gift into the fireplace.

I gasped and took a step back as sparks leaped into the air. Crackling flames engulfed my precious present.

"I don't take pleasure in this, Millie," Mother continued, reaching for the cupcake. She pulled off the paper. "You bring this upon yourself."

Then Mother ran a finger through the icing and sucked it clean. "Delicious." She licked the cupcake clean of icing then tossed what was left into the flames now devouring my present.

I stepped back, horrified. If only there wasn't something wrong with me. But I didn't know how to be better. I swallowed the lump in my throat.

Mother came to me and tucked my shoulder-length hair behind my ear. "There, there, darling. You have another birthday in a year. That gives you time to think about how to obey. And I'll be here every day to remind you who you are. Fair enough?"

I nodded, and Mother patted my shoulder. She walked past me and spoke over her shoulder before she left the room. "Remember, this is all because I love you."

I watched the fire crackle for another long moment as Mother's heels clicked away. My lip quivered and I stifled a cry, feeling as worthless as Mother said I was.

Overwhelmed with guilt and sorrow, I hurried back to the safety of the attic, tears running down my cheeks. I cried into my pillow for a while before exhaustion put me to sleep.

Knocking woke me a few hours later, and at first I wondered if I was in a dream. Mother would never come knocking so late at night.

Tap, tap, tap.

There it was again, and I was definitely awake. I pushed myself up, frightened. The sound came from the opposite wall. There wasn't anything on the other side of the wall except the outside world.

Wind sometimes rattled two loose boards in the drafty attic, but this noise resembled a tree branch knocking against the house. I considered this. No tree grew on that side. So what was it?

Tap, tap, tap.

I glanced at the clock: 11:00 p.m.

Tap, tap, tap.

Did woodpeckers peck at night? I didn't think so. Either way, there was no way I could sleep through the ruckus. I mustered some courage and crossed the room, eager to shoo away whatever creature was invading my space.

Tap, tap, tap. Tap, tap, tap.

I knocked against the wall with my knuckles and the rapping stopped. Relieved, I turned away.

Tap, tap, tap.

Frustrated now, I spun back and dug at the edge of the loose board. The six-inch plank popped open, allowing cold winter air into the room. I did the same thing to the board directly underneath it, creating a gap in the wall large enough to poke my head through.

The moon was bright, illuminating the soft snow falling from the sky. I turned my head toward the sound and saw a small woodpecker had dug its tiny talons into the panels. It twisted its neck to look at me, then launched from the wall and flew downward.

Straight down to the shoulder of someone who stood in the fresh snow, staring up at me.

I gasped. It was the old woman Aggie, the only person I knew who didn't live on the property. I'd met

Aggie while doing chores near the fence. It was as if she'd called me out with the help of a woodpecker. How was that possible?

Her short, wild white hair and bright-blue eyes caught the moonlight. She was wearing her customary homemade cloak and black hiking boots.

I'd overheard Martha say no one knew where she'd come from or where she lived. The woods, some said. She'd been born to wolves and lived alone deep in the trees. She was a hermit who could talk to animals. She hunted people who got lost in the woods. She was crazy.

But on the handful of occasions I'd interacted with Aggie, I'd never seen anything that made me think she was crazy. She was funny, saying things that didn't really make sense, often whispering to the foraging squirrels and birds. But she was also kind. Her eyes shone with excitement when she spoke, and her laugh was delightful.

Mother forbade me from speaking to her, so I tried my best to stay away. But here she was, looking up at me in the middle of the night. I wasn't even sure how she'd gotten past the tall iron fence that surrounded the property. If anyone spotted her and reported it to Mother or Mr. Pruitt, they'd be furious.

"What are you doing?" I whispered down, knowing

she probably couldn't hear me. But I couldn't risk being heard inside the house. "You shouldn't be here."

In answer she flung something from her hand, and I watched the object fly toward me before slowing and falling back to the snow. A stone? What was she doing?

She snatched it up and looked at me, making sure I was ready. She threw it again, harder, and this time I caught it with both hands. I pulled it inside. A folded piece of paper had been tied to the rock's surface.

Untying the twine, I pulled the folded paper free and opened it under the bright moonlight. There on the white page was a note.

> *Millie Maven, I have long awaited this moment.*
>
> *On this day of your 12th birthday I would like to offer you a way to change your life forever. To have the life you were destined to have. A life with wonder and power beyond your wildest imagination. You have been chosen to follow a special path. You may decide, but it must be tonight, before your birth date passes.*

Meet me outside where the five tall pines stand. You may be afraid, but don't let that stop you, my dear. You must come! If you don't, you'll be trapped in that house forever.

My heart was pumping hard and I read the note again. What could this mean?

I looked down, disbelief still swimming in my mind. Aggie motioned for me to come, then turned and walked west, in the direction of the pines.

She couldn't be serious! She wanted me to follow her? Break Mother's rules and sneak out? I watched her for another moment and then quickly replaced the boards, struggling to get the nails to line up with their holes. Satisfied they would hold unless a strong wind came, I crossed back to my corner.

Paper still in hand, I read the words again. Then again, reminded that these were words written by a woman most thought was insane. The ramblings of an old loon who lived off pinecones and talked to birds. But my heart began to beat to a different rhythm as Aggie's words sank into my soul.

You must come! Your future depends on it.

Could it be? It must be! How did Aggie know it was

my birthday anyway?

I sat there, staring at the note, caught in a war between my mind and my heart. One moment my thoughts dashed the song of my heart, and then the next my heart soared over those thoughts, drawing me to Aggie.

I stood. I had to know what Aggie meant.

I donned all the clothes I owned to battle the winter night, yanked on my shoes, and crossed to the steps in the floor. With a huff, I shook off my fear and opened the hatch.

CHAPTER THREE

The front door would expose me, so I slipped out a window in a vacant bedroom on the main floor. My feet touched down in the cold packed snow, and I turned away from the house. It had stopped snowing, and the moon seemed brighter above the blanket of white. A shiver ran down my spine. I would be easily spotted out here.

The five pines were a good way off. Embracing a surge of courage, I raced toward them. The full moon illuminated the white ground and, though glad for the light, I wished I had some cover as I crossed the wide-open lawn.

My chest was heaving when I finally reached the trees. The iron fence was only ten paces farther and beyond that, the dark forest.

"Hello?" I whispered.

Nothing. Dread filled me. What if Mother had used Aggie to tempt me to leave?

"Psst."

I jerked my head to the sound and saw Aggie emerging from the dense forest beyond the fence. Relief washed over me.

"Come, we must be quick," Aggie said. She stepped up to the fence and dropped to a squat. "I've been working on your escape."

She scooped out a massive heap of leaves, revealing a small hole. Had she prepared this escape route earlier? I glanced over my shoulder to make sure we weren't being watched. The mansion sat like a monster eyeing me. I saw the clear trail I'd left in the snow. Too late.

I turned back to Aggie, who winked and motioned for me to come.

"Wait," I said, filled with more fear than I could shake. "What is this?"

Aggie looked down and then back at me. "This is a hole," she said, eyebrow cocked.

I wasn't amused. "That's not what I meant."

She smiled, charmed by herself. Her eyes sparkled in the night. "This is the path to a whole new way of being, my dear Millie. A way to freedom from the trouble you fear. A way that will change your life forever."

"I don't understand."

"Do you know who you are, Millie Maven?"

The sting of Mother's words echoed in my head. "Yes," I said softly. I knew exactly who and what I was. "Mother says I'm a mistake."

"Wrong!" Aggie said in a loud, funny voice. I snapped my head to look over my shoulder, afraid someone might hear.

I turned back. "You don't even know me!"

"Wrong again. I do know you, child. And I've been waiting for you to be ready to see for yourself. You've been chosen."

That word again. If she knew me really, she would know there was no way a girl like me could be chosen. Yet something deep in my gut pulled me toward the hope she offered. The same feeling had pushed me out of the attic.

"Come with me," Aggie said, "and you'll find wonder beyond your wildest imagination."

"Mother will be furious."

"On the contrary, she would insist. Your real mother, that is, not the woman who parades around pretending to own you."

"You knew my mother?" I asked.

She nodded. "I knew the day she went missing that you and I would be standing here tonight."

I blinked at her. "My real mother isn't missing," I said. "She's dead."

"Are you certain about that?" Aggie asked calmly.

"Yes," I said, but the challenge in her eyes made me hesitate.

"If you insist." She smiled at me. "You remind me of her, you know. The same eyes, the same nature. The same bright spirit that Priscilla Pruitt has tried to snuff out. But I tell you this: as certain as I am standing before you, not everything is as it seems. Listen to the calling you feel and come with me, Millie. You are special. Let me show you."

My mind raced with possibilities and questions I couldn't easily put words to.

"The choice is yours, Millie Maven," Aggie said, tearing me from my thoughts. "Go back to the life you know or follow me to a new life. Don't worry, you'll be back before the sun rises. Not likely the same person, mind you, but you'll be back if that's what you want."

I looked back at the dark mansion again. "You promise I'll be back before the sun comes up?" I turned back to her. "I can't risk Mother finding me gone. You have no idea what price I would pay."

"Promise," she said. Then repeated, "If that's what you want."

"It is," I said.

"There you have it."

I'd already come this far. As long as I got back before being discovered, there would be no trouble.

Pushing away my fear, I dropped to my stomach and started to wiggle through the hole Aggie had made. It took some effort, but then I was through.

I'd never been outside the fence. For a moment I felt giddy. I really was free, wasn't I? At least for a moment.

"Come, we must go," Aggie urged, starting off into the trees.

I followed as best I could as she picked up her pace. She knew the terrain, but it was all new to me. I stumbled and nearly lost my footing more than once. I tried to stick to her exact route, but only filtered moonlight cut through the branches.

"Keep up, child," Aggie chuckled. "You're stronger than you think."

I pushed my legs harder, testing their limits. We twisted through the trees. Branches caught my clothes and snow crunched under my feet. I was out of breath when we burst into a deep sandy canyon with towering cliffs on either side. The sight of such massive rock structures stopped me in my tracks. I'd never seen anything so magnificent.

"Hurry," Aggie said. "We only have until midnight."

"Midnight for what?" I asked, stumbling after her toward the far cliff wall.

"For you, Millie. For you!"

We approached a large boulder at the base of the cliff, and behind the boulder the cliff face was cracked. A fissure two feet wide split the rock wall from top to bottom.

Aggie stepped up to the crack.

"We're going in there?" I asked.

"We are," Aggie said. "It's the only way."

My stomach dropped. A distant wolf's howl echoed through the canyon and my fear spiked.

"I will be with you the whole time," Aggie said. "There's nothing to fear here."

Except being eaten by wolves. Like the ones that had raised Aggie. Maybe the old woman lured little girls into dens like this to feed the wild animals. Girls foolish enough to follow her. But my heart chased away the whispers of my mind, and I followed Aggie as she entered the cave.

"Hold on to me. Don't let go," she said.

The crack widened and allowed me to walk beside Aggie in pitch darkness, gripping her elbow. I have no idea how Aggie found her way as she led me deep into that cave, but she didn't trip or stumble once.

I don't know how far we walked. It seemed to be forever, but in that darkness, my mind played tricks. Maybe only five minutes had passed when she finally pulled up.

"Wait here," Aggie said, stepping away from me.

"Aggie?"

"I'm here. Just wait."

Thirty seconds later, a flame sprang to life. Aggie had put a spark to a torch on the wall, and the moment it flared three others came to life, two on the opposite wall.

We were standing near the edge of a pool brilliantly lit by the four torches. It glowed from a light source deep within.

"Magic," I whispered.

"No, not magic," Aggie said. "They're all connected. Now the water . . . Well, some might say there's magic in the water, but I can assure you there is no magic in this world. There is, however, the power of the Great Teacher. His ways are mysterious and marvelous. You will see."

My eyes fell to the pool of blue-green water, which rippled as if a light breeze swept over its surface. But the air around me was still. A light mist or steam rose from the water. Maybe it was a hot spring.

"What is it?"

"It's what I've been waiting to show you since the day you came to live here in Paradise," Aggie said.

I couldn't pull my eyes away from the water. There was something deeply mysterious about it.

"You were chosen to take the same journey of discovery all are called to, Millie," Aggie said, her voice now soft. "Unfortunately, few actually take it. I'm here to give you a boost of sorts. A little help for a girl who's lost her way. You don't yet see the truth of who you are, but here, through these waters, you might see a different way if you are willing."

I crept closer to the pool's edge as if pulled by an invisible force.

"All you must do is accept this call and dive deep into the pool," Aggie said.

Her words jarred me. "Dive?"

"Yes, dive. To a place where anything is possible."

I was too shocked to respond. What exactly was Aggie suggesting?

"Think of it as your imagination, a place with no

limits," she said. "Where possibilities are endless and power vast."

I faced her. "Like a dream?"

She dipped her head. "If you like."

"Is it real?"

"Real is what you make it, child. But the effect will be real, that much I can assure you. Real, real good. Would you like that?"

Excitement buzzed under my skin. "Yes."

"Of course you would." She took a deep breath, eyes on the water. "But with great wonder comes great danger. You will face what you fear most, but it's worth it, my child."

"In the water?" I asked. It seemed preposterous.

"Not *in* the water," she said. "*Through* the water to the light beyond. There, the ways of the Great Teacher will be made known to you. There, you will see everything that blocks your sight of who you really are as one born into the light of the Great Teacher."

"Who's the Great Teacher?" I asked.

Aggie's face brightened. "He's the reason you're here. He's the one who gave everything so that you might know the way to his heart, the place where there is perfect love."

"I don't understand."

"But you will. And you will know him."

I looked back at the pool. "I'll drown."

"No, you won't, but if you're too afraid, then I'll escort you back to the Pruitts' home. This choice must be yours and yours alone."

"How long will it take? I can't hold my breath very long. And you know I have to get back before Mother discovers I've gone."

"Once through the water, time changes. One day here might be a week beyond the pool, so you'll have plenty of time. There's nothing to fear. Nothing here, that is."

"A week? How will I know when to come back?"

"Well, these things aren't precise, but if you insist on being back before sunrise—"

"I do."

"—just make sure to return within five or six days there. That should do it."

"Five or six? What if you're wrong?"

"Then make it five just to be sure."

I couldn't possibly do what she was suggesting, but something in the water refused to let me turn my back. Was it as warm as it looked?

Dive to the light or return to the life I'd always known—those were my choices. I didn't want to go back to the cold attic. To Mother and her disapproval. To Mr. Pruitt and his hatred. To my own self-loathing. Pain and loneliness waited for me there. Could there be more through the water?

"Time is running out, my child," Aggie said. "You must decide."

"And you'll be right here, waiting?"

"Yes, of course. Right here waiting. Just enter the water and swim for the light, then do the same to return. Everything else will become plain. Oh, there is one more thing. Once through, you may not remember this world. But that's of no consequence. Dive, my child. Life awaits you."

It didn't occur to me then that if I couldn't remember this world after entering the water, I wouldn't know to come back in five days. But I was too distracted by the wonder of the water itself. I had to know.

Stepping toward the pool, I stripped down to my simple white dress and long socks. I set the rest aside and walked to the water's edge.

"You're sure?" I said absently, looking for one last word of assurance.

"I have no doubt."

I looked back at the water and stepped in, gasping as warmth spread up my ankles. It tingled with power unlike anything I'd ever felt. As I waded in, the water rose to my knees, then waist, then shoulders, and my fear slipped away.

I took a deep breath and dunked my head. The power was all around me, humming in my ears and reaching to my bones. I opened my eyes and saw that the brilliant blue-green color surrounded me. Beneath my feet, a pocket of shining white light beckoned. I dove for it, pushing my hands through the water and kicking my legs to propel me.

The pocket grew and my lungs started to burn. Maybe I should have been afraid, but I wasn't. The white light blinded me to all the other colors. Bright, hot light wrapped around me, erasing everything else.

And then everything went dark.

CHAPTER FOUR

I startled awake and jerked up. Where was I? In a dim room with musty air. After blinking hard, my eyes started to adjust, and I realized I was sitting on a wooden floor. It felt rough under my fingertips and was covered in a dirty film. Behind me was a wood-paneled wall that curved up to a beamed ceiling.

I shivered, noticing my white dress was damp. My hair too. Wet socks, tall to my midcalf, covered my feet, but I wasn't wearing shoes. But that was because I'd gone into the pool and ended up . . .

Where was I? Was this a dream? Sure didn't feel like one. My arms were covered in goosebumps and I rubbed them. I definitely wasn't dreaming. So what was I doing?

I pushed myself to my feet and scanned the room. Barrels as tall as my shoulders stood along the left side of the room in six clusters of twelve. Stacked crates, too many to count and all different sizes, lined the opposite side from floor to ceiling. Between was a narrow misshapen path that led toward a short staircase. Light filtered in from the square opening at the top of the steps.

I took a step and only then noticed the room was swaying ever so slightly. Like a ship. This had to be a ship. What was I doing on a ship?

I tried to recall exactly what I'd been told by . . . That was odd. I couldn't remember the old woman's name. The woman who'd led me to the pool where . . .

But then I couldn't even remember what I'd done at that pool. Or what the woman had looked like. Or even if there really had been a woman. Maybe that was all just part of a dream and I was home.

Was this home? Why couldn't I remember anything about this place?

I took several steps along the path as my brain churned. I ran through the things I *did* know. My name was Millie Maven. I was on what seemed to be a large wooden ship. I had come through a pool. Or had I? I couldn't remember the place I'd come from. My mind was simply blank.

My heart pounded. I had no recall at all of anything

before waking up. Not even a hint. *I have amnesia*, I thought.

Who was I?

I carefully climbed the steps, passed through a narrow hatch, and emerged into a thin hallway. Six feet to my left, the hall turned a corner and opened into a large room filled with people.

I stopped as all eyes in the room flicked to me. Twenty or more kids about my age sat on long wooden benches in front of me. Boys and girls watched me stand there like a statue.

"Hello there," a warm voice said to my left. I flinched and twisted to see a short old man with thinning white hair, wire-rimmed glasses, and bright-blue eyes standing beside me. He was wearing navy slacks and a matching long-sleeve tunic that hung to his thighs. His feet were bare.

Beside him stood two older kids, a boy and a girl, teenagers by the looks of it, both in identical light-gray uniforms. Their faces were stern as they watched the children. Guards, I thought. Why would these children be guarded?

The old man offered a comforting smile. "It's alright. You're safe. And you're the last one to arrive. Welcome. Please join the others, will you?" He gestured to an open spot on the rear bench.

I turned to him. "I can't remember how I got here," I whispered, aware that everyone was still watching me.

He nodded. "It's alright, everything will be explained. Please, sit."

His face was warm, and his presence felt too comforting to be dangerous. So I did as he asked and took the empty spot at the back. The old man walked to the center of the room and smiled at us all.

"I know you have many questions, and I promise they will be answered when we arrive shortly," he said. "Please keep your silence and follow instructions, and all will be well." Then he turned and ascended the staircase behind him.

"Hey," someone whispered beside me. The girl had fiery red short hair, perfect cream skin, and golden freckles. Her hair looked nearly dry, but dampness spotted her jeans and green T-shirt. Had she also come through a pool? I glanced around and noticed many of the others looked to be damp as well. Had all of us?

"Any idea where we are?" she asked. "I can't remember anything."

I opened my mouth to answer—

"No talking," the male guard said, expressionless and cold. The female guard stared at me and I looked away, not wanting to cause trouble.

This room was like the one I'd woken in but taller, with wood-paneled curved walls on both sides and thick wooden beams holding up the ceiling.

My eyes flickered to the others around me. I counted fourteen boys and ten girls of various ethnicities. I couldn't see many faces because I sat on the last row, but I could feel their uncertainty and fear as strong as my own.

My mind raced over a few worst-case scenarios. I'd been kidnapped. I'd been in an accident or poisoned and suffered from permanent amnesia. I'd broken a law I couldn't remember, and this was my punishment. I was going to die. There was no way around it—I was done for.

For a long time I rehearsed these scenarios as the boat slogged through the water. There had to be other possibilities. More hopeful ones that I couldn't think of.

The boat slowed and the hull bumped against what I assumed to be a dock. We had arrived. To where I had no clue, but I was desperate to know.

"Alright!" the boy guard barked. "We do this quickly and on my order. One row at a time, single file. Here to my left are boots. Grab a pair quickly, go up these stairs onto the main deck, and then to land. No talking. Let's go."

The front row moved as ordered, heading first to

the pile of rubber boots. One by one each grabbed a pair and were ushered up the steps. When my row stood I followed the redheaded girl. I was the last in our line and the only pair left looked too big for me. I grabbed them anyway and followed the others up the stairs to the main deck, where I squinted under bright, hot sunlight.

"Put on your boots and follow us," the older boy said. "Be quick."

My toes swam in the oversized footwear. I followed the group off the ship, down the dock and onto shore, where I pulled up at the back of the procession. We looked like a small troop of prisoners being marched to our fate. But maybe that was just my fear talking.

Still, I didn't know who we were or what we were capable of. Maybe I was right to be afraid. I glanced back and saw the large-sail ship, like an old Spanish galleon I'd seen in a history book. Behind it, the water stretched to the horizon, crystal blue and clear. Fifty paces ahead of us, the strip of beach ran into a dense forest.

"Listen up," the lead guard's voice called. I could hardly see him through the heads of those gathered in front of me, and I pushed on my tiptoes to get a better view.

"Stay together, eyes forward," he said. "Don't wander off. Let's move!"

I was the last to take a step, the sand crunching beneath me. I looked for the kind man who first greeted me but didn't see him anywhere.

My mind teetered on the brink of terror and hope. I wasn't the only one who couldn't remember anything. The redhead had said she was confused as well. So we were all in it together, and that was my hope. It couldn't be that bad if we were all in the same pickle, right?

But not knowing anything is its own kind of fear, and I was swimming in it.

We left the beach and entered the forest. It was difficult to keep up in the oversized boots, and the group was slowly pulling away from me around a bend. The toe of my left boot caught something jutting out of the forest floor. I fell to my hands and knees.

The last of the group was just stepping out of sight. I let out a heavy sigh and pushed myself back to my feet.

"You alright?" a voice asked.

I twisted and saw a tall muscular man in plain jeans and a white button-down shirt standing beside a large oak tree, arm cradling firewood. His eyes were piercing green and he offered me a soft smile. He seemed kind, different from the guards.

"You took quite a fall there," he said.

I felt my cheeks flush. "Yeah, I'm okay."

He nodded. "Well then, you'd better catch up."

He was right, but I wondered if he could shed some light on what was happening.

"Do you know where we are?" I asked.

He chuckled and gave a small shake of his head. "Right, you can't remember. Don't worry, that's just part of the game they play. It'll be okay, just stay with your group."

I hoped for more, but it didn't seem like he was going to share.

"Oh," I said. "Okay, thanks." Then started forward.

"Do you want some advice?" the man asked.

I stopped and faced him again.

"You seem like a sweet girl, so just be careful who you trust. Not everything in this place is what it seems."

What did he mean by that? "Am I in danger?" I asked, but before he could answer someone else's voice cut through the trees.

"Hey, you!" a female voice called. The guard had come back for me. "What are you doing?"

I was confused for a moment. Surely she could see what I was doing, but when I glanced back at the man, I noticed he was tucked behind the oak tree and the guard couldn't see him. I opened my mouth to explain, but she interjected first.

"Get back here with the rest of the group."

The man gave me a small nod before disappearing into the woods.

"Hurry up," the girl called again.

The woodsman's warning hung in the air. *Not everything in this place is what it seems.*

I pushed forward, working to keep my feet under me as a new sense of dread opened in my chest.

CHAPTER FIVE

We walked through the woods for a good twenty minutes, my mind tumbling over my encounter with the stranger, wondering if maybe I should have gone with him. Wondering who I was blindly following and why.

Why couldn't I remember anything about where I'd come from or who I really was?

We finally stopped at the edge of a vast rolling meadow. The male guard directed us to spread out in six lines, four to a line. His golden hair shone bright in the sun and I could see the blue of his eyes. He'd seemed menacing in the boat, but here in the light he looked kind enough. Maybe the guards weren't really guards.

"My name is Roger Goss, but people call me Riggs," he called out, pacing with his hands behind his back. "This here is Chaplin Lane." He pointed to the female guard standing toward the back of the group.

"I was just like you once. I arrived here, with no memory of where I'd come from, afraid and confused. So was Chaplin. Both of us have been in your shoes. Saplings, noobs, first-timers. Neither of us were aware of what we were capable of, but we learned. If you're willing, you will too. And let me tell you, saplings— what comes next is going to rock your world."

A smile crossed his face as he started walking backward, arms spread. "Welcome to FIGS."

He turned and took several long strides. The golden field began to change. One moment the field was empty, but as Riggs crossed some kind of invisible barrier, the air shimmered and our eyes opened to a new view.

The field became a large property, home to a massive castle-like structure half a mile away. A vast lawn stretched toward us in waves of perfectly cut green grass. A wide dirt road lined with tall, thick willow trees cut the land in two. It was hard to make out details of the castle, but I could see spires that reached up to the sky on either side, dozens of windows that dotted the stone walls, and massive wooden double doors.

The sight took my breath away.

"This is FarPointe Institute for Gifted Students," Riggs started, "otherwise known as FIGS, and if you're lucky you'll end up inside. But that isn't where your journey begins."

Riggs drew my eyes back to him as he headed to our left. "Follow me," Riggs called, and we hurried behind like a small flock of sheep.

My mind was still reeling as Riggs led us down a slope. I stole more than one look over my shoulder to see if FIGS actually had appeared out of thin air.

It was still there. Amazing!

A few minutes later we topped a small hill and saw a large campsite in a shallow grassy valley. To the north, more rolling fields. FIGS was by now long out of sight.

I counted thirteen white canvas tents, tall and wide, lining a manmade pathway, six to a side. The thirteenth tent, the largest by far, stood at the campsite's head, with two big firepits burning on either side of the tent's open entrance.

Riggs led us down toward the camp as four people emerged from the large tent. They were adults, men and women, and all wore dark-blue uniforms. They took their positions between the firepits. Their faces were gentle and kind and generally smiling when we finally stopped in front of them.

Our escort formed us up, then joined them. The man to Riggs's right was the one who'd greeted me on the ship. He caught my eyes and gave me a kind wink. It made me smile. Maybe I was safe after all.

From the main tent emerged a striking woman in white, her braided silver hair hanging to the middle of her back. She had dark-brown skin, sharp cheekbones, and caramel eyes. A beautiful emerald medallion, the size of a half dollar, hung from a gold chain around her neck.

"Welcome to FarPointe Institute for Gifted Students," the commanding woman said. "My name is Kyra. I'm dean of FIGS." Her voice was strong but welcoming. She motioned to the others. "You've met our Leads support team, Riggs and Chaplin. They are students who completed the program and returned to offer their services. And these are our professors."

She motioned toward the elder farthest to the right. "Professor Claudia," Dean Kyra said. The short round woman smiled and gave a tiny wave. She had thin lips, wide eyes, and a grandmotherly look.

"Beside her, Professor Tomas." The man was average height, tanned, and bald. He gave us a single nod.

"Professor Alexandria," Dean Kyra said, motioning to the next in line. A tall, broad-shouldered woman with blond hair and stern eyes. She didn't smile or nod, and I was already worried about interacting with her.

"And last but certainly not least, Professor Gabriel, whom you met on the boat," the dean said. The man placed his hand over his heart and bowed.

"A pleasure to see you all again," he said as he straightened, adjusting his glasses. I liked him very much already.

"You will get to know them each more later." Dean Kyra crossed her hands behind her back. "For now, we will start at the beginning. Raise your hand if you remember being transported here through a pool?"

Everyone raised their hands.

"Keep them raised if you can't remember anything before that," Dean Kyra said.

No one dropped their hand. I looked around at the faces of the kids I could see. A shorter boy beside me, pale and blond, had worry in his eyes. Another girl in front of him, with dark skin and black hair pulled tight atop her head in a bun, wore uncertainty on her face. A girl taller than the rest with black hair, the ends dyed hot pink, bangs nearly covering her eyes, oozed fear. Each one of us was just as unsure and frazzled as the next.

"Don't be afraid; your minds are just fine. Memory loss is an essential part of the program. Your memories were taken to give each of you a fresh start. No histories, no *ideas* about what you are capable of. Here you will discover something new. However, you will find you still have all your fears, joys, and preferences. Your personalities are intact. You are still you, just without any history—without the stories of where you came from and who you are. In that way, you are all the same. Starting from the same place."

The words of the woodsman echoed in my mind. *It's part of the game they play.*

Dean Kyra stepped toward us and made direct eye contact with each person.

"You are special. Each of you holds potential far beyond your imagination. This is true for every living child, but your being here in this special place is a unique opportunity. You've come to us because, although you don't remember it, you hope to discover your true potential through the lessons you will learn in the world of FIGS."

She paced back, studying us carefully.

"We refer to the unique potential in each of you as gifts. Here at FIGS, those gifts give you the ability to do things you may have once thought were impossible. Like this."

Dean Kyra closed her eyes and everything was still for a moment. Then I felt the ground moving. Several students around me gasped as the grass at our feet began to grow. The blades shot up, fast and thick, brushing against my legs and then my waist, then over our heads. We instinctively moved closer to each other, staring up in amazement. The grass grew until it blocked out the camp, a forest of impossibly tall grass too thick to part.

My pulse beat in my ears as we all stood close, too shocked to move. I wanted to pluck a blade and examine it, but it started to return to the ground. Shrinking as quickly as it had grown, it was soon just regular grass again.

"I have a Nurture gift," Dean Kyra said. "Every child has gifts, and our first purpose here at FIGS is to awaken those gifts in you."

"Are they like superpowers?" a small redheaded girl blurted, the same girl I'd sat next to on the ship.

Dean Kyra gave her a small smile. "They are simply gifts, my dear, given to us by the Great Teacher for the sake of all. Your true superpower is to change hearts, not make grass grow. Make no mistake, your true power doesn't come from any parlor trick. In the end, it's all about your heart. Do you understand?"

"Yes," we muttered, though I wasn't sure.

"Who's the Great Teacher?" a smaller boy with blond hair asked.

"The one who gave his life so you can find true life,"

Dean Kyra answered. "The one who teaches not simply through words but through the heart."

Now that questions were being answered, half of the kids began asking questions at once.

"Students, students, please," Dean Kyra said, reducing the boiling chaos to a simmer. "I promise all your questions will be answered in time. For now, we focus on what is directly in front of us."

She cleared her throat, back on track.

"Good." Dean Kyra dipped her head. "Now, in the world of FIGS there are three categories of gifts: Strength gifts, Transformation gifts, and Nurture gifts. Each category has its own varieties. For example, Strength gifts may present as brute strength or great speed."

The kids around me started to whisper.

"After your gift makes itself known, you will receive a bronze medallion at a ceremony. Its bronze color will change to reflect your category." She held up her own bright-green medallion. "As you can see, Nurture gifts are emerald. Strength gifts are gold, and Transformation gifts are sapphire."

"How will you wake up our gifts?" someone asked.

Dean Kyra placed her arms behind her back and paced right. "Starting today you will undergo three challenges. These challenges make up what is known as the Initiation Trial, which I will explain after you get a good meal in your bellies."

The tallest boy in the group looked back toward the castle and asked, "When we get our gifts do we get to go to FIGS?"

Dean Kyra smiled. "Before you can move into FIGS, you must complete the Initiation Trial. These three challenges will present more than a little danger, as you will see. At any point, you may decide to end your training and return to the place from which you came. There is no shame in that. It only means you aren't ready to take this particular journey."

Dread filled my gut. I was probably going to be one of those. I couldn't remember who I was, but I knew for sure I wasn't very brave.

"But looking at this group, I'm willing to say we may have the strongest bunch to ever set foot on FIGS grounds. I can sense it in my bones."

Her words lightened my worry a little.

"Before we continue," Dean Kyra said, "the Leads will show you to your sleeping quarters, give you clean clothes, and take you to the mess tent. You must be hungry after your journey, and you will need your strength for what comes next. It is a pleasure to finally have you here, and I look forward to watching each of you grow."

CHAPTER SIX

We were divided into groups. There were three sleeping tents for the girls on one side of the path, and three for the boys directly across. I followed Chaplin into one of the girls' tents. She pointed me toward a cot.

The tent was large enough to fit a dozen cots but had only four. Tall wooden stakes held up the white canvas walls. At the back were two private spaces for changing and two full-length mirrors.

Chaplin faced us. "As you know, my name is Chaplin." She was average height with black curly hair that cascaded around her collarbone and framed her dark eyes. "I'll be in charge of the girls' tents." She wore a medallion like Dean Kyra's, except it was sapphire.

"As I told the other girls, you will find clean uniforms

on your beds, as well as sleeping clothes and new boots. You have been assigned a bed. Please do not switch or I will switch you back."

I decided it was in my best interests to do what I was told.

"I'll give you a minute to settle and get dressed. The mess tent is the last on the right side. I expect you there in fifteen minutes," Chaplin said. With that she left the tent, allowing us all a moment to catch our breath.

A mousey girl with long wavy brown hair and a button-shaped nose sat on the cot across from me. She barely glanced up at me and I knew she was terrified. I turned to see several uniforms folded on my bed. Dark-grey, cotton, with long-sleeve tops and matching pants. Black boots would serve as my footwear. Everyone else had the exact same thing.

I changed quickly and then sat on my bed, waiting for the others. I didn't want to walk to the mess tent alone.

"Hey there," someone chirped beside me. The redheaded girl sat on a cot to my left. She was already changed as well. "Remember me?"

She didn't let me answer before continuing.

"Man, this is crazy, right? I mean . . ." She mimed her brain exploding as she made the sound effect with her mouth.

I smiled. "Yeah."

"I'm Mackenzie, but friends call me Mac." She paused and squinted her eyes. "I mean, I think."

"I'm Millie," I said.

Mac nodded. "I'd ask you where you grew up, but . . ."

I got it. We were strangers to ourselves almost as much as we were to each other. Except I still sensed certain things. Like when I felt I probably wasn't ready for the danger Dean Kyra said we would face. Or like now, sitting in the tent, watching the girls talk, the scene felt foreign, like it was something I hadn't experienced. Dean Kyra had said we still had our fears, joys, and preferences. That our personalities were intact. Maybe these feelings were a clue to who I was. If so, I didn't like the picture I was getting.

"We should go," Mac said. "Wanna walk together?"

I nodded and stood. It felt nice to have someone close. I liked the twinkle in Mac's eyes, the way she smiled with ease, like everything was going to be okay. I was thrilled she was here with me. We walked to the mess tent and Mac chattered the whole way.

I wonder what's in there. I hope our tent is nicer than the boys'.

I keep thinking about my family. Is someone wondering where I am?

You think this is all real, right? What if we're all having one big collective dream?

Is that even possible?

I didn't respond to any of her questions, because I don't think she was looking for answers. She was just putting her thoughts out there. They filled the silence as we collected our lunch of grilled chicken, peaches, and cheesy cauliflower. We sat to eat.

The mess tent was filled with picnic tables, five or six kids to a table, all of us in dark-grey clothing. The chatter was soft, most unsure what to say, others asking questions no one could answer.

A chubby boy sat down next to me, frowning at what was on his food tray. He looked up at me, his moppy brown hair hanging into his dark matching eyes.

He shrugged and asked, "You think it's too much to ask for pizza?"

Mac giggled from across the table and I felt myself smile. She started to say something, but Dean Kyra walked into the tent, drawing the chatter to a hush.

"I hope everything tastes alright and that you ate your fill," Dean Kyra said. I glanced at the boy beside me as he tried a bite of chicken and then pushed his tray away. Mac put her hand over her mouth to muffle her laughter, and I bit the inside of my lip to not smile. For a split second, I thought everything was going to be okay.

"Because the first trial begins right now," Dean Kyra said.

My hope vanished.

CHAPTER SEVEN

We followed Dean Kyra out of the mess tent to a small rise. She turned toward us and waited for us to gather close. The late afternoon sun was sinking fast, and a chill in the air brought me a sense of foreboding.

"As I said before, the purpose of the Initiation Trial is to reveal the gift inside of you," Dean Kyra began. "The Initiation has three challenges. This first one will test your physical fortitude. Will your gift manifest when you find yourself in physical danger? We're about to find out."

Fear worked its way up my spine. Physical fortitude? I was small and felt weak.

Dean Kyra continued. "But first, some things to be aware of: this is your challenge alone. You may not assist anyone. Should your gift manifest, use it to complete your task."

She lifted the emerald medallion that hung around her neck for us to see.

"Your purpose now is to discover your gift. The medallions are not your gift, nor do they have power by themselves. But make no mistake, the medallion we give you will be valuable indeed. Do you follow?"

Nods all around. Satisfied, she released her medallion.

"If you complete the task without your gift manifesting, you won't receive a medallion. If you do not complete the task, you will not receive a medallion. The only way to receive a medallion is to discover your gift. Am I clear?"

"Yes," came the responses, hesitantly now.

"Good," the dean said. "Don't worry. Each of the three challenges will present you with the opportunity to manifest your gift."

Her voice became more somber.

"If you do not receive a medallion by the end of the Initiation Trial, your time at FIGS will come to an end. You will return to your old life with no memory of being here."

Worried whispers broke out. For reasons I couldn't

comprehend, I was afraid of going back. Terrified even. But why?

"There's one more important factor to keep in mind," Dean Kyra said. "You may use anything you find to help you. I recommend you look for two items in particular: white diamonds and black onyx. We have hidden several of these stones in locations that will seem out of place to you. Look for what doesn't belong. One will guide you and the other will protect you, and you will need them for the third challenge."

I could feel the anxious energy of the whole group.

"In challenge number one, you must get off the island before it sinks," Dean Kyra said. "May your gifts manifest. May the Great Teacher guide you."

The world around us shifted. Just as when FIGS appeared from nowhere, the air shimmered and the scene changed. One moment we were all standing before Dean Kyra, and the next we were huddled together in the middle of a jungle.

Chaos erupted as kids tried to understand what was happening. Some froze; some cried out.

"Listen up!" Mac shouted. "This is a challenge. A puzzle. Don't panic. We just need to solve it." She seemed so confident and I felt so afraid.

With that Mac took off south, cutting through thick

foliage that towered over me. As if on cue, most of the others scattered in different directions, leaving me and maybe eight others in the small clearing.

I thought to stumble after Mac, but my feet were rooted to the dirt. What now?

"Hey." Mac's familiar voice came from behind me. I spun around to see her stumbling back through the thick underbrush, her eyes wide with worry. "Come look!"

A brother and sister who had to be twins rushed up to Mac.

"What?" they asked in unison, which gave me the creeps. Both twins were tall with pale skin and raven hair. The girl's hair hung dead straight. Her brother's was tied in a low ponytail at the nape of his neck. Both had the same blazing blue eyes.

"Follow me," Mac said and hurried back the way she'd come.

We all followed, pushing our way through, nearly toppling over one another. No more than fifty yards in, the dense underbrush dumped us out onto a narrow beach that stretched in both directions. Behind us, the huge tangle of jungle loomed dark and threatening. Ahead, waves crashed on the sandy shore. No more than fifty feet beyond those waves waited the mainland, our destination.

"We can swim across!" a boy yelled and ran toward the water. He dove into the waves, but the moment his body entered the water, the waves spit him back onto the shore, where he landed in a heap with a sharp cry. The water seemed to be alive! The boy stood, soaked and coughing, shaken but not broken. Not this time anyway.

"Of course, it wouldn't be that easy," the twin girl bit off.

"It was worth a shot," the soaked boy snapped back, but I could hear the embarrassment in his voice.

Water touched my toes and I looked down to see the waves were closer than they'd been a moment earlier. I had been standing at least two feet from the water.

Mac noticed too, as did several others.

"Get off the island before it sinks," she said, repeating Dean Kyra's words.

The water was its own kind of monster, reaching in to feed on the land and anyone on it. As the urgency of our predicament became clear, chaos returned.

"What are we going to do?" the still-sopping boy demanded.

"Would they really let us drown out here?" cried another.

The twins started off to the west.

"Where are you going?" Mac yelled after them.

They turned back. "No assisting each other," the girl said. And then without missing a beat her brother added, "Only the strong survive." They shared a twisted smile and dashed off. Everywhere around me others started doing the same.

My mind tumbled over itself. *This can't be happening,* I kept thinking. *This isn't happening.* A hand grabbed mine and yanked me back toward the jungle. It was Mac.

"Come on, Millie."

I ran into the dense growth with her, back through where we'd arrived and beyond to the other side of the island. Thick leaves and vines pulled at my arms and face. The ground was uneven and webbed with huge roots. Mac was faster than me and I struggled to keep up. I knew I was holding her back and thought she'd be better to leave me behind.

Thunder deep enough to rattle my bones crashed above the trees, and lightning flashed in the darkening skies.

I stumbled and slammed into the ground, scraping my palms deep enough to draw blood. I gasped in pain. If I had any doubt before, it left me now. This was real!

I was really bleeding and if I didn't get off this island I would really drown.

"Millie," Mac cried. She crouched to help me up as another flash of lightning and roar of thunder pierced the sky.

"Seriously?" Mac screamed at the air. "Just give us a break!"

"This island's gonna kill us," I said, panting.

"We're not powerless, remember. I mean, if we have these gifts like Dean Kyra—she can control the earth or whatever—then we have something too. Right?"

"But how do we know if we're ready?"

Mac opened her mouth as if to answer but didn't have anything to say. We knew nothing. They had thrown us all into the lions' den without teaching us how to tame lions.

As if mocking us, the sky bellowed, and a jagged streak of light struck a massive tree with enough power to cut it in two. The towering top half fell toward us.

"Mac!" I screamed, scurrying backward. My heel caught on a root, and I toppled feet over head down a steep slope. I tumbled over, grabbing for anything that would stop me.

Finally I crashed to a stop, knocking my shoulder against a large boulder. Tears stung my eyes but I didn't have time to dwell on my pain. Time was running out!

I pushed myself up as the sky dumped sheets of rain. I looked up the steep hill, searching for any sign of Mac.

"Mackenzie!" I cried. The wind blew rain into my eyes and I wiped them clear. "Mackenzie!" Nothing.

I was alone now. I was weak and alone in a terrifying challenge that required me to be strong. Which meant I was dead meat.

I pushed away images of Mac being smashed by the fallen tree and tried to focus.

Okay, this is a test. Get off the island, Dean Kyra said. So there has to be a way to do that, right? Mac had said we weren't powerless, but that's how I felt in that moment.

Some of you aren't ready for this yet. Dean Kyra's words echoed through my head.

Only the strong survive, one of those eerie twins had said. That truth rooted me in place. But I had to try.

I was standing up to my ankles in shallow water. Glancing around, I saw the jungle floor covered with rising water. Could I really drown out here?

Fear gripped my heart. I had to get to higher ground!

The slope I'd crashed down was too steep and wet to climb, so I raced along the base and prayed I'd discover a way up. Darkness was falling fast. The rain poured and the sky continued to illuminate the island with flashes of lightning. My chest heaved as I sloshed through water that now rose to my calves and soaked my pant legs.

I was about to turn back when I spotted a way up the slope. The route ended at a ledge. Pushing myself harder, I started up, using my hands, gripping wet roots and digging my fingers into the mud.

I ignored the pain pulsing in my bloody palm as I reached the top and grabbed a sharp rock on the ledge. With all the strength I could muster, I hoisted myself over the crest. I rolled onto my back and faced the sky, panting as the rain soaked my face.

The water was rising and I wouldn't be safe here for long. I had to keep moving!

Thunder shook the ground as I hauled myself to my feet and stumbled through crowded trees. I squeezed and maneuvered through the tight spaces, praying to break through.

Bark and branches tore at my arms, cut my shirt, and formed bruises and small cuts on my legs and upper body. I pushed on blindly and finally burst into a small clearing. That was good!

But water flowed over the ground, rising by the

second. And that was bad. Very bad.

"No, no, no," I cried. I rushed through the clearing, thinking I had to find higher ground. Maybe Mac was there, at the highest place. If not her, someone had to be.

But I didn't find it. Instead, I found myself at what was left of the shore. I say left of it because the shore was mostly under water now. Everywhere I looked I saw waves crashing, eating away the ground and pulling trees into the water. I was stuck. My mind had run out of ideas. There was no hope.

My body took over then, and without thinking I tore back into the trees even though I knew there was no sanctuary there. The island had beaten me. I had no gift to get me out of there. I was going to drown.

Water rose past my knees. The whole island had been transformed into a swamp and would soon be swallowed. Rushing was pointless, but I rushed anyway.

I finally slogged back into the small clearing, and there I stopped. As the rising water lapped and swirled around me, all I could think was that this is exactly what I should have expected. I wasn't strong enough for FIGS. That must have been something I knew in my other life, something I couldn't outrun even here. I didn't deserve a gift or a medallion. I wasn't like the others. I wasn't special like Dean Kyra said.

The water rose past my thighs, flooding as if a dam had broken. Within seconds it was up to my waist. My whole body shivered violently in the freezing water. I was going to die. This was the end.

"Help!" I screamed. "Help!"

Did I know how to swim? I couldn't remember but I flailed as the water surged up to my chin. Then over my head. And I discovered that I couldn't swim.

The ocean swallowed the island and took me with it. All my strength left my body. I went limp and let myself sink like a stone beneath the waves. I was drowning in the deep black vastness of the ocean.

I was starting to lose consciousness when an invisible force wrapped itself around my middle and yanked me from the waters. My body broke the surface and I inhaled, rough and desperate. Air filled my lungs.

And then I passed out.

CHAPTER EIGHT

When I came to, I was lying facedown on a thick bed of grass. Alive! I lifted my head to see I was in the same field we had been led to before the island trapped us. The storm was gone. Sunset painted the western horizon orange and pink. My clothes and hair were soaked, and a breeze chilled my damp skin.

I sat up slowly, and that gentle movement confirmed my body had taken a beating. All the students were back, some standing around chatting as if their lives hadn't just been threatened, others soaked and shaking their heads, others dazed and pale like me. The professors stood to one side, watching us and talking with students.

Pain pulsed through my hands, and I examined the cuts in my palms. Maybe we couldn't die in the trials, but we weren't safe at all.

"Millie." Mac hurried toward me. She reached for my arm and helped me to my feet. "I tried to find you!" She glanced at my bloody hand. "Those cuts look pretty bad."

"Yeah. But I'll be okay," I said, shivering.

Mac bit her bottom lip and glanced around to see who was listening. "Something unbelievable happened to me." Before Mac could explain, Dean Kyra raised her voice.

"May I have your full attention, please? Gather around."

We all moved toward her, but a hand lightly tapped my shoulder. I turned to see Professor Gabriel offering me a thick wool blanket. His white hair shone against the pinks of the sunset, and he gave me a warm smile.

"You alright?" he asked softly.

His presence was so comforting I wanted to melt into tears. I wanted to say no, I wasn't alright. But I couldn't do that, so instead I just accepted the blanket.

He glanced at my bleeding hands. "May I help you with those wounds?"

I extended my right hand and he hovered his palm over it. The dark forest-green medallion around his neck caught my eye, and I realized what he intended to do.

I nearly backed away, but something that felt like warm water surrounded my hand, soothing the pain. A moment later when he moved to my other palm, the cuts were completely gone. Healed right before my eyes!

I must have looked shocked, because he said, "It can be alarming at first, but you'll get used to it. If you need anything, come find me, okay?" Professor Gabriel held my eyes with such genuine kindness I knew he meant what he said.

"Okay," I said.

"Good." He gave me a gentle nod. "Good." And then he stepped toward the other professors.

I hurried toward the huddle, staring at my healed hands, then hastily shrugged into the blanket Professor Gabriel had given me.

At the front of the gathering, the dean cleared her throat. "You have finished the first challenge of your Initiation Trial," she said. "Well done. I know for many of you this feels like a failure. It is not. Two challenges remain, and with each new test you will have a new opportunity to find your gift. Often in times of deep suffering we discover our strengths. No need to be discouraged."

But I did feel discouraged. Deeply. If the island was

any indication of what was to come, I was toast.

"Some of you excelled in this first challenge," Dean Kyra said. "You can feel your gift expanding even now as you begin to express what has always been in you." She looked across the group with a proud expression. "When I call your name, please step forward to receive your medallion."

Professor Claudia, holding a humble wooden box, took her place beside Dean Kyra, who lifted the lid and reached inside. "Dash Elite," she said.

I watched as the tall pale twin with long black hair approached, his sister grinning proudly.

Dean Kyra pulled out a plain bronze medallion, motioned for Dash to extend his hand, then placed the medallion in his palm. She closed his fingers around the object and then cradled his hand between her own.

"For the gift of Strength, I present you a gold medallion. May you discover its power and align to it in fullness. May your intentions be good. May your heart be strong."

She released her grasp and Dash smiled widely as he unfolded his fingers. The plain bronze medallion was now glistening gold. Students gasped as another impossibility came to pass right before our eyes.

"I can feel it," Dash said in awe.

"Of course you can," Dean Kyra said. "It comes from within you. Here you will learn to use it wisely. Please step back."

He did and Dean Kyra continued. "Doris Elite."

Dash's twin sister stepped forward. Dean Kyra placed another plain medallion in her hand as she had with Dash. I wondered what the twins had done to earn their gifts. Had they escaped the island with those powers? I assumed so but didn't know. Mac might.

Dean Kyra spoke to Doris for all to hear. "For the gift of Transformation, I present you a sapphire medallion. May you discover its power and align to it in fullness. May your intentions be good. May your heart be strong."

Doris held out a brilliant-blue medallion, her face beaming with pride.

"Congratulations," Dean Kyra said. "Please join your brother."

Everyone was watching the dean, eager to see who else earned medallions. Maybe all of them but me.

"Adam Kirkplin," Dean Kyra continued. I watched as the boy the water had spit back onto shore stepped forward and received a silver medallion, also categorized as a Strength gift. Same gift, different paths, different abilities. Then a girl named Collene Hall was given a deep forest-green medallion, a Nurture gift, which I knew was a healer gift because Professor Gabriel had the same one. All medallions came out of the box plain and took on new color in their recipients' hands.

Dean Kyra scanned the students. "Mackenzie Spitzer."

Mac glanced at me with a small smile as she went to the dean.

"For the gift of Nurturing, I present you with an emerald medallion. May you discover its power and align to it in fullness. May your intentions be good. May your heart be strong." Dean Kyra smiled brightly, holding Mac's eyes as she added, "Welcome to the club."

Mac grinned as she revealed a beautiful emerald medallion matching the one that hung around Dean Kyra's neck. They shared another knowing look before Mac returned to my side. I could feel my stomach slosh with jealousy and tried to keep it from my face. I was happy for my friend, but it was hard to feel that joy through my self-pity.

Professor Claudia closed the box and withdrew. That was it, only five students. The rest of us had failed. Honestly, that gave me some comfort. I wasn't alone. Not yet anyway.

"Those who have received your gifts will feel them

grow within you. For now, using your gifts outside of the challenges is strictly prohibited. Until you learn to use and control them, you could be a danger to yourself and others. Any misuse of your gifts will result in consequences. Do you understand?"

The five medallion holders nodded.

"Those who have not yet received your gifts, do not give into self-doubt. Instead, focus on the voice deep inside you that calls you to your gift. That voice will never lead you astray. I will see you tomorrow."

With a nod from the dean, Riggs and Chaplin directed us back to camp for dinner. The professors watched in silence as we took our leave.

Back at camp, we were instructed to change into clean clothes and head to the mess tent for our meal. I obeyed in a bit of a fog. I felt totally lost here. I was a complete failure who was sure to be sent away.

CHAPTER NINE

In the mess tent, everyone was pounding the medallion recipients with questions. How they got them, what their gifts did, how they discovered them. We gathered at a few tables in the middle of the tent. I would have sat next to Mac, but she was surrounded by admirers, so I ended up at the end of the table, half a dozen kids between us.

Adam's silver medallion was for speed. He'd run across the top of the water to escape the island. Dash had jumped far enough across the water in a single bound to land at safety. His sister had transformed the water into ice so she could walk across it. Collene had healed a massive bird that then flew her off the island.

I was amazed by the wild tales, and I longed to have one of those abilities. I was also afraid of what I might have to risk to get it. If I even could.

Mac had stopped the falling tree from crushing us, then realized she could control nature. Using her gift, she'd fashioned a bridge over the water from the tallest tree near the coastline.

With each account and each tidbit of new information, my desire for a gift grew. So did my shame for being so weak. They'd all done incredible things. Dean Kyra said that same potential was inside me but I doubted it. Then again, it had happened for Mac. Maybe it could happen for me too.

The chubby boy from earlier joined me. His name was Boomer Talley.

"You want that?" he asked, pointing to the piece of chocolate cake untouched on my dinner tray.

"No," I said. "Go for it."

He smiled and snagged the cake. The conversation died down some as kids started to clump into smaller groups. With a happy sigh, Mac plopped down next to me. "Crazy day, huh?"

"Yeah, crazy," I said.

Boomer looked at Mac hesitantly and asked, "Can we see it?"

Mac smiled and pulled out the half-dollar-sized emerald medallion. Boomer and I both leaned in to see it up close. It shimmered in the light, looking like it was cut from a single gemstone. An image of a large oak tree encircled by an intricate design of woven vines was etched into its surface. I reached out to touch it and glanced at Mac for approval, which she gave with a nod. It was cool to the touch, smooth like metal, and I thought maybe I felt a pulse of something quiver under my fingertips.

"Each medallion has a picture engraved in it," Mac said. "Dash and Adam have a mountain. Collene and I have trees. I'm not sure what they mean."

"What does it feel like?" I asked.

Mac exhaled as she thought about it. "Like both lightning and calm are trapped inside me. Like my skin is buzzing but my mind feels steady."

"How did you know to use it?" Boomer asked.

"I didn't know. I just reacted, and it came from me like it was always there, and I had just—"

"Awakened it," I finished.

She nodded at me, then placed her hand on my arm. "You'll know what I'm saying when it happens to you." Her eyes seemed so clear and hopeful. It was contagious. She believed in me, so maybe I could too.

"Mackenzie," a voice called, and we turned to see Dash and Doris standing at the end of our table. My eyes locked with Doris's and a shiver passed down my spine.

"You should keep better company," Doris sniped,

followed by Dash as if they shared the same mind: "Not everyone will find a gift," he said. "Some will fail."

They both glanced from Boomer to me and I could feel my cheeks redden.

"Who made you two authorities on anything?" Mac fired back.

"We have feelings about these sorts of things," Dash said.

"We're never wrong," Doris agreed.

Mac frowned. "Well, you're going to be wrong this time."

"You're wasting your time, Mackenzie," Doris snapped, and her brother completed her thought: "You could be with us."

"You don't know me," Boomer said, timidly glancing up at the twins. I could see his fear but also his anger.

Dash and Doris shared a pitying smile. "No," Dash chuckled. "But we can see you."

"And seeing you tells us all we need to know," Doris said.

Boomer pushed back from the table and stood, his anger breaking through his fear. Dash stepped forward a few inches in front of his sister, so he was closer to Boomer than seemed safe. For Boomer.

"What are you going to do, fatty?" Dash taunted. "I have a medallion and you have nothing."

Boomer dug his hand into his front pocket. "I have this," he said, yanking out a small black orb the size of a ping pong ball.

The scene had drawn a small audience and we were all looking at the strange stone in Boomer's palm.

"And what's that supposed to be?" Dash asked.

"It's one of the hidden stones," Boomer said.

Mac gasped and smiled as she stood. "I totally forgot about those! You found it?"

In the chaos of trying not to drown, I hadn't even thought to look for the things Dean Kyra had said could help us in the last test. Judging by the looks on the others' faces around us, I guessed I wasn't the only one.

Boomer locked eyes with Dash. "So I have something you don't. Guess that makes us the same."

Dash looked as if Boomer had spat in his face. Doris stepped up, her eyes narrowed to slits.

"We are not the same," Doris hissed.

A moment later Boomer yelped and glanced down at his hand.

I followed his look and saw that the black orb had become a puddle of melting glass. Boomer started screaming as it charred his flesh, and other students started to panic.

Riggs burst into the mess tent and rushed over.

"What's going on?" Riggs demanded. Boomer was still crying, and Riggs grabbed the boy's wrist.

"Chaplin," he called and the other Lead entered the tent. She saw what had happened, placed her hand over Boomer's steaming palm, and closed her eyes.

A moment later Chaplin removed her hand and the black orb was back in its original state. Underneath it was a deep red burn mark on Boomer's palm. Riggs carefully lifted the orb as Boomer sobbed.

"Get Professor Gabriel," Riggs said to Chaplin. She gave a nod and left.

"I can help," Collene said, stepping forward. "I have a healing gift too."

"No!" Riggs snapped. "Did you not hear Dean Kyra? This is exactly why using your gifts is forbidden outside the challenges."

He moved his eyes to Doris. She was the only one with a Transformation gift, and Riggs knew it. "You should be thankful it only burned him."

Doris's face reddened, but I could feel her embarrassment. "He threatened me and my brother," she barked, pointing her finger at Boomer.

"Threatened you?" Mac snapped. "He didn't threaten you."

"He did," Dash said, stepping forward. "I was there."

"I did not!" Boomer protested, through tears. "You burned my hand!"

"Quiet!" Riggs yelled. "I'll be keeping this." He placed the orb into his pocket.

"That's not fair," I blurted out. I swallowed, surprised by my outburst as Riggs looked up at me, his eyebrows raised, waiting for me to continue. "I mean, it's not Boomer's fault. He was just sticking up for himself." Somewhere in my mind a small voice was telling me I should stop talking, but I didn't. "If anyone's at fault it's the twins. Doris broke Dean Kyra's rule."

I could feel the eyes of the Elite twins on me, hot and hateful.

"You're right," Riggs said after a moment. "You five will meet with Dean Kyra in the morning and we'll let her decide how to handle this. Trust me, it won't be nearly as simple as losing an orb." His tone held warning, and I realized I may have gotten us all in more trouble.

"Everyone to bed," Riggs ordered. "Now."

The room emptied quickly. Doris knocked me on the shoulder as she passed, Dash on her heels.

"You were invisible to me before," she hissed. "Now I see you. Big mistake."

Dash drilled me with dark eyes and then the

two of them stormed out.

Professor Gabriel pushed into the tent and toward Boomer. "Oh dear." He took the boy's hand. "No worries, you'll see." A moment later Boomer's palm was back to normal.

"All better?" Professor Gabriel asked, examining the hand through his glasses. Boomer nodded with a sniff and the kind professor tapped the boy's shoulder. "To bed then."

"Come on, you three," Riggs called. "Let's go."

We went. But I was even more afraid now.

CHAPTER TEN

In my dreams that night, I stood outside a large mansion shadowed with dark clouds, covered in menacing points and sharp edges. A crow cawed on the roof and then flapped into the sky. *I know the huge house*, I thought. But I didn't know it, if that makes sense. I couldn't place it. But there was no doubt about one thing: this was a bad place.

A very bad place.

I shivered in the cold and noticed I was wearing my thin white dress. My feet were bare and my hair was damp. The crow sang again, a terrible song that made my heart jump. I didn't know where I was or how I had gotten there, but every bone in my body screamed *run*.

The wind picked up, whirling around me and cutting at my flesh. It had frozen the ends of my hair and stiffened my dress. I heard whispering. A haunting tone that came from nowhere but felt like it was all around me.

"Millie."

I spun, searching for the speaker.

"Something's wrong with you, Millie."

The woman's voice flooded my ears and I jerked my head back and forth looking for the source. But I was alone with the daunting, dark house.

"You're just an ungrateful, worthless girl. You should be ashamed. There's something wrong with you, Millie."

Over and over the whispers came, stabbing my soul. I clamped my palms over my ears, trying to block out the voice.

"You should be ashamed. You bring this on yourself. You're a foolish girl. Be better than who you are. Can you do that, darling? Can you be more than weak? More than worthless?"

My whole body tensed as shame consumed me. I dropped to my knees, desperate. The wind's intensity grew. It was a monster intent on devouring me whole.

The voice turned bitter. *"Ungrateful, worthless girl! Be better than you are! Be better! Worthless, worthless girl."*

I sprang up in bed, gasping at the night air. It took me a moment for my mind to remember where I was and for my eyes to adjust to the darkness. I was in my bunk at camp. I could hear the deep breathing of the other girls, and I began to settle. Just a dream. But so real!

I took several deep breaths, trying to ignore the echo of that voice in my ears. *There's something wrong with you, Millie. You should be ashamed.*

Shaking my head, I yanked back the sheets that covered my legs and swung them to the ground. I ignored the chill, slipped my feet into my boots, wrapped myself in the robe we'd each been given, and crept from the tent. The firepits on either side of the main tent still burned with bright-yellow flames. The bathrooms, one marked for boys and the other for girls, were only a dozen paces from where I stood.

The night sky was bright and clear, the stars and moon providing light as I headed toward the girls' bathroom tent. I pushed through the closed flap. An oil lamp lit the room. I just needed to splash some water across my face to wash away my nightmare. I didn't know who the voice belonged to, but I couldn't avoid the familiar dread it opened in my gut. I should know a voice from my past.

I patted my face dry and was hurrying back to my tent when motion caught the corner of my eye. I turned to see a man loading firewood into one of the pits beside the main tent.

He looked up and I saw his face in the firelight. It was the woodsman. We stared at each other for a moment, then he finished his work and headed out between the tents.

I stepped after him, then stopped. What was I doing? He was a stranger and it was the middle of the night.

Well, he wasn't a *complete* stranger. And he was feeding the fire, so maybe he worked at FIGS. He must. I found myself wanting to speak with him again.

Careful who you trust, he'd said. *Not everything is as it appears.* What had he meant by that?

Against my better judgment, I followed him around the tents and saw a soft glow over a small knoll. Another camp?

The moonlight lit the way over the knoll, where I stopped. The woodsman warmed himself by a small fire next to a single-man tent. As I headed toward him, I wondered if he was a groundskeeper.

"You should be in bed," he said without turning around.

"I couldn't sleep," I replied.

He finally turned, his eyes darkened by night. Flames flicked shadows across his face. "You shouldn't be wandering around alone at night. It's not safe."

It wasn't? For a moment I considered running back, but I didn't want to, not yet. Instead I stepped closer to the fire's glow.

"You didn't tell me you worked here," I said.

He shrugged.

"What do you do?" I asked.

"Little things, here and there. Mostly I watch the grounds, make sure little girls who sneak out of their tents don't go missing."

He was teasing me, but his words unnerved me anyway.

"Why can't you sleep?" he asked.

I could lie, but something made me want to tell the truth. "Nightmares."

"Hmm," he said with a frown. He took a deep breath and motioned me to sit. "I have something that might help with that."

I moved into the firelight and sat on the fallen log where he pointed. He ducked into the tent, rummaged for a moment, then returned with a small glass jar and a metal kettle. After filling the kettle with water from a large drinking pouch, he hung it over the blazing fire and then sat on another log across from me.

"What was your nightmare about?" he asked.

I wasn't sure I wanted to tell him. I felt embarrassed.

"No need for concern. Dreams can be windows into our minds. Maybe I can help you understand what it meant. My grandmother interpreted dreams. She taught me to do the same."

I hesitated another moment, then lowered my eyes to the fire and told him about my dream. Where I had been, what it had looked and felt like, the storm that had been brewing. "And there was a voice," I said.

"What was it saying?"

"Terrible things," I whispered, looking up at him. "But maybe true." Emotion gathered in the back of my throat.

The man held my eyes for a long moment and nodded. I thought I could see kindness in his face.

"I'm sorry," he said. "That sounds awful."

"Do you know what it means?"

"Well, sounds like a warning of something dark to come."

"Like what?"

"It could be anything. Dreams aren't an exact science, but in my experience, it usually has to do with something you already fear. And voices . . . as terrible as you say it was, it sounds foreboding."

A warning against something that was coming. Something I was already afraid of? "The second test," I whispered.

"You're right to be afraid," he said, as he checked the water inside the kettle. "There are dangers lurking here where you least expect it." He looked away and shook his head. "I'm sorry, I shouldn't be talking to you about this."

"Why not?" I asked.

"It isn't my place. Besides, my own experience would probably do you no good."

"So, you've been around when the other groups come through?"

"Many." he said. "And there will always be more." His face looked sour in the firelight, as if he'd suffered some great injustice.

"You can tell me," I said. "I promise to listen."

He smiled. "And I promise to never lie to you." He considered his words before he spoke again. "So, I'll just say this: don't ignore the warnings. The voice that speaks to you is often wisdom trying to help you see who you are."

His words resonated deep within, and I watched him as he poured steaming water into a wooden mug, added a spoonful of the mixture from his glass container, and stirred.

He handed the cup to me and I accepted it with a smile. It was warm against my hands and smelled like cherries. "What is it?" I asked.

"Something my grandmother used to give me to help me sleep. It works quickly, so you should take it back to your tent. You can keep the mug. I make them when I need a distraction. Each is made from a single piece of maple."

"It's nice," I said, turning the cup in my hands. It was only half full. Must be strong stuff.

"Drink it all and you'll sleep like a baby," he said.

I stood to do as he said. "Thank you. I don't even know your name."

"I'm just an old woodsman."

"Nice to meet you, woodsman. I'm Millie."

"You should go back to bed, Millie," he said. "I'll walk you."

I turned and started back toward camp, the woodsman following a couple steps behind. I was glad for his protection. We didn't say anything until we were back at the edge of camp.

"Thanks again for the tea," I whispered.

He dipped his head. "If you need more, I'll be around."

I headed for my tent. After a few paces, I glanced back and saw that the helpful woodsman was gone. I snuck back to bed, downed the warm tea, and within minutes was dead asleep.

CHAPTER ELEVEN

I stood with Mac and Boomer inside Dean Kyra's tent. Dash and Doris stood to our left, glaring. The five of us had been summoned after breakfast and asked to wait inside.

From the outside, the tent looked identical to the others, just larger. But inside it was lavish. Beautifully colored rugs covered the floor, different ornate tapestries hung against the canvas walls, and two thick curtains of purple material divided the space in half. I couldn't see behind the purple barrier, but I imagined it was grand.

The front section of the tent was filled with comfortable sitting cushions, a plush cream couch and matching chairs, a small but well-stocked bookshelf, a mahogany coffee table with thick curved legs, and a large polished-wood desk that reflected the silver chandelier above it.

We stood waiting for several minutes, avoiding eye contact with the twins, feeling the heat from their death stares. Beside me, Mac was starting to squirm.

The purple curtains swayed as a hand parted the center. Dean Kyra stepped through and sat at her desk, facing us. I swallowed my anxiety and tried to remain positive. Dean Kyra seemed fair. Surely she would see that Doris and Dash were to blame.

"Have a seat," the dean said, glancing at us. We all settled onto the big cushions.

Dean Kyra interlaced her fingers and placed her hands on the top of her desk. "I hear the five of you put on quite a show during dinner last night."

None of us spoke.

"I understand how difficult this transition can be and how emotions get involved as you navigate a new environment," Dean Kyra started in her ever-calm delivery. "However, we expect our students to abide by the rules. And the rules were broken last night. Thankfully, no one was hurt. Things could have been much different."

I hoped Dash and Doris were about to get what they deserved.

"Because you were all involved, it's only fair you all face consequences," Dean Kyra said.

"What?" Mac exclaimed.

"We didn't do anything," Boomer objected.

"You attacked us!" Doris barked.

"We were just defending ourselves," Dash added.

I'd thought Dean Kyra would see our side. Why were we all getting in trouble for something that had been done *to* us? None of us had used our abilities. Boomer and I didn't even have gifts yet. It wasn't fair.

When the objections ran out, Dean Kyra continued. "Everything here is about learning. All of you played a part in this incident, so you will all learn from it. I hope. You're embarking on a journey that should unify you, not divide you. At FIGS, we believe in supporting one another and working together. No one student stands above the rest, a lesson from which you all could benefit."

Mac leaned forward. "Dean Kyra—"

"My decision is final," the dean said, standing from her desktop to stare down at us. "In the next challenge the five of you will each face more difficulty than the others. Should your paths cross, you have permission to offer one another help, but only if it's in your heart to do so."

Dread filled my gut. She was adding difficulty to the second challenge. If it was anything like the sinking island, the last thing I needed was for it to be harder.

"Look at this as an opportunity for growth," Dean Kyra said. "I will see you all for the second challenge."

She walked to Boomer and held out the black stone he'd found. "I believe this is yours."

He took it and tucked it back into his pocket. Dean Kyra walked back through the purple curtains. We stood and made our way outside. Most of the others were still in their tents.

Doris stormed past me, leading her brother, who glared at me. If looks could kill, I would have been dead on the spot. I didn't want to be afraid of the twins, but I couldn't deny the way they made my heart race.

"This is unbelievable," Mac mumbled beside me.

Boomer joined. "I should've kept my mouth shut."

I shrugged. "It's my fault. I made things worse."

"No way," Boomer said. "You were sticking up for me like a good friend is supposed to."

A bell clanged overhead, drawing others from their tents.

"Alright, line up," Riggs yelled, appearing from my right. He looked down at me and gave a small wink. "You know what that sound means, don't you?" He answered his own question before I could.

"It's time for the second challenge."

✦

We followed Riggs and Chaplin out of camp and through the woods toward the south, walking in a long single-file line. A few hundred yards on, we emerged from the trees into a large golden wheat field with stalks tall enough to brush the sides of my arms. At the center, dark against the bright grain, stood a monstrous wood house.

I stopped cold and Mac bumped into me.

"Ouch," she objected. "What the heck, Millie?"

I didn't respond. I couldn't. I just stared at the sight in disbelief. It was exactly like my dream. Ominous and threatening, as if I got too close it would open up its front doors like jaws and swallow me.

"You okay?" Mac asked, pulling me from my thoughts.

I swallowed. "Sorry, I just feel like I've been here before."

"Really? Weird," Mac said.

"Yeah." I nodded, the words from the woodsman echoing in my mind. *Sounds like a warning of something dark to come.* This was definitely something dark. Had my nightmare been a foreboding?

I wanted to run. Disappear into the tall wheat. All

the fear and pain from the last challenge came rushing back. I wasn't sure I could do this.

We were brought to a stop in front of Dean Kyra and the four professors, who stood in front of the horror house.

"Welcome to your second challenge," Dean Kyra began. "A challenge of the mind. Because of the difficulty of this challenge, you will enter in pairs."

My heart rate eased and I smiled at Mac.

"Except for the five students who met with me this morning," Dean Kyra continued, looking at us. "You will enter alone."

My comfort vanished.

Dean Kyra pressed on. "Again you have the opportunity to find the black onyx or white diamond stones. Seek them out. They will be extremely helpful in the final challenge."

"What if we already found our gifts?" Collene asked. "Do we still have to go through the challenge?"

"Yes," Dean Kyra said. "Though the purpose of these challenges is to awaken your gifts, if you have already done so there are still things you can learn inside each challenge. You may use your gift if it is available to you."

She pointed to the front door. "You will enter the house and face the challenges within. The house will decide what obstacle you face. Your only objective is to find the way out."

"No, no," someone was muttering at the back of the group. I turned to see small Peter, I think his name was, shivering and pale.

"I can't do this."

"Are you okay, Peter?" Dean Kyra asked kindly.

Peter looked panicked. "No," he managed. Then louder, "No, I won't. I can't! I'm too afraid."

The dean spoke gently. "I urge you to—"

"I don't even want a medallion!" Peter said, backing away from the group.

"Wuss," I heard someone whisper.

I glanced toward the voice and saw the twins smirking. Doris lifted her eyes toward me and slowly mouthed, *You're next*. I was grateful for the way Mac had her arm looped through mine. She was my anchor.

I glared as hard as I could, but inside I was as unnerved as Peter. Maybe a medallion wasn't worth it.

"You said some weren't ready," Peter said. "I'm not ready. I want to leave." His voice cracked and I knew how hard he was trying not to cry.

Dean Kyra walked up to Peter and placed her hand on the boy's shoulder. "You must understand, young man, that fear is a natural response to the unknown.

If you can trust you will be safe, I can assure you that tomorrow will bring new emotions."

"No," Peter said. "I don't want to be here tomorrow. I don't even know who I am or what I'll go back to, but it has to be better than this."

He voiced a struggle that I imagined many of the others had. At least they didn't fear going back. Me? I was sure that whatever I'd left behind was full of darkness, which left me torn between two bad options: staying and leaving.

"Are you sure that is your choice?" Dean Kyra asked.
Peter nodded.

"Then I wish you the best of luck, young Peter," Dean Kyra said. "May I see you again." She nodded at Riggs, who escorted Peter back toward the forest. And beyond that forest, the sea. Back home.

Leaving was that easy. You could just walk away at any moment.

"Does anyone else feel they're not up to the challenge?" Dean Kyra asked.

Part of me wanted to rush forward and declare I wasn't ready. I didn't want to face what my dream had warned was coming. I was afraid of the twins and the forest and everything about this place.

But the fear I felt when thinking of the life I couldn't

remember kept me silent. So I would stay. Mac would help me. And I had Boomer, who was a real friend as well, right? The woodsman was helping me. Professor Gabriel said he would help me. Or at least they would try.

"Very well then," Dean Kyra said. "Let us begin."

CHAPTER TWELVE

"Remember, all you must do is get out of the house," Dean Kyra said. "First pair, step forward."

Riggs and Chaplin had paired most, leaving Mac, Boomer, Doris, Dash, and me at the end of the line in a single file. One by one, pairs ascended the stairs and entered the front doors of the monstrous house. Mac nodded back at me when it was finally her turn, then walked up and was gone. When the door opened I tried to catch a glimpse of what was inside, but all I saw was darkness.

Dean Kyra motioned me forward. "May the Great Teacher guide you, Millie."

I took a deep breath and stepped inside. The door clicked shut behind me, and for a moment there was only darkness. Four lanterns made of black iron flickered to life, one on each wall, and were soon blazing.

The room that came into view was lined with shelves built into the walls. Rows and rows of books. From floor to ceiling, shelf after shelf, hundreds of books.

A library.

I looked back, expecting to see the door, but another wall of books had taken its place. Every inch of wall space was covered.

The room was a perfect square, maybe fifteen feet wide, with a ten-foot round maroon rug covering most of the floor. I scanned the shelves, searching for anything other than spines, but there was nothing. It was eerily quiet, except for the soft crackling of flames and my pounding heart. I was alone inside a library with no entrance. And no exit.

Dean Kyra had said this was a challenge of the mind. It had to be a puzzle then, and I needed to find clues that would help me escape. Dust covered the books. Their spines were red, brown, orange, and green. Their titles were hard to make out in the lamplight.

I stepped up to one of the walls, held my breath and gingerly touched a red spine. Nothing happened. Nothing on the next one either, or the one after that. Running my fingers along the spines, I felt for a clue to what I should do next.

Nothing.

I glanced around the room again. What if I couldn't figure this out? My pulse beat faster. What if I was terrible at puzzles? How could I know when I couldn't even remember who I'd been before coming here? I'd been too weak and too slow to succeed at the first challenge, and maybe now I was too dumb to complete this challenge.

My breathing became heavy, and I closed my eyes to regain my calm. *Focus,* I thought. *Focus, Millie. Go slow and see everything.*

I studied each row of books carefully. I went around the room twice. It wasn't until my third pass that I noticed something unique. The color of the spines seemed to form a pattern. A brown spine, then green, orange, and finally red. Different shades, but the same color family. That had to mean something. I followed the pattern around the room.

Brown, green, orange, red. Brown, green, orange, red. Brown, green, orange, red. Brown, green, red . . . I stopped.

Red! Following the pattern, the book should be orange. It was out of place. I pulled the book from its place and opened it. A small rectangle had been carved out of its pages, and in that hollowed space sat a brass key. My heart jumped.

I yanked the key and stared at it in my trembling fingers. I had to figure out what to do with it, but at least I'd made some progress. I was elated!

I was about to close the book when I saw the writing on the inside cover. *Uncover to find what has always been.* I read it again under my breath.

Something clicked softly and the room began to rumble. I jumped back as the wall to my right jerked and began to slide inward. Toward me. Startled, I glanced around and saw the opposite wall also moving, narrowing the room. Both walls moved about a foot before stopping.

Maybe that was it. Ten seconds passed, and then the soft click sounded, and again the walls slid in unison. They were closing in on me and I'd already wasted time! Panic clouded my logic. I took a calming breath. *Think, Millie. Think!*

If the room narrowed a foot every ten seconds . . . I had to get out, and quickly.

Uncover to find what has always been the inscription had said.

"Uncover what?" I started yanking books off the shelves. I uncovered nothing. The walls continued to move. The lanterns swung with the movement, and the flames inside began to snuff out, sending sections of the room into darkness. *There is nothing else here*, I thought, *and I don't have enough time to rip every book off every shelf.* I had to be missing something.

Uncover to find. What could be uncovered? The floor vibrated as the walls slid toward my small frame. I trembled in my boots.

I gasped. My boots. Under my boots lay the rug, books strewn about, the creeping walls pushing up the edges on either side. "Uncover," I said. I began kicking books off the rug, as many as I could. I grabbed the front edge. The rug was thick and heavy and I had to use both hands to yank it far enough back to see what it was covering.

There, in the middle of the floor, sat a small trap door, secured by a padlock.

I dropped to my knees, acutely aware that the walls were closing in on me. Time was running out.

I fumbled with the lock, desperate to shove the brass key into the keyhole. The walls rattled closer, shaking the floor with such ferocity now that I dropped the key.

"No!" I cried, digging at the key to peel it off the floor. I tried the lock again. Fear blinded me as the walls squeezed the room, now no more than six feet wide.

The key slid into the lock, and with a twist it sprang open. I tore the metal mechanism from the iron loop it had secured and yanked up on the heavy wooden door.

A narrow wooden ladder stretched down into pitch darkness.

Somewhere something popped, and all four lamps snuffed out. Time was out.

Pushed by panic more than thought, I madly felt for the ladder, grasped the top step, and swung my feet into the opening just as the closing walls reached me. I flung myself down, clinging to the ladder.

Careful with my foot placement, I descended. Six rungs down, just enough for my head to clear the floor, a terrible crack exploded in my ears. Small wooden fragments rained down on me as the closing walls above shattered the trap door.

That could have been me!

I clung to the ladder in the darkness and sucked air into my lungs, safe. But now what?

I eased down the ladder and found the floor with an outstretched foot. The darkness was thick, but I could feel a light breeze behind me. Turning slowly, I felt for something to hold onto in the passageway.

My fingers touched rough, cold walls. Stone, I thought. Same on the other side. The dark space was barely the width of my arm span. I reached up to feel the same stone only a foot overhead.

I kept my hands on the sides as I slowly advanced. Something scurried next to me, its tiny nails scraping along the stone floor. Forcing away thoughts about what kind of creatures lived in the passageway, I picked up my pace.

The tunnel curved to my right and ahead I saw the first gray of light. It was only a glimmer, but in that dark space, even the faintest of lights was enough to make me want to scream with joy.

I was going to make it out!

Using the wall to my right as a guide, I picked up my pace. Then I was jogging. And then I was at the exit, a narrow opening crowded with vines and leaves. It took me only ten seconds to tear the foliage aside and stumble out into open air.

Now I did scream for joy. Maybe it was more like a whoop than a scream, but I was out! I'd made it out!

Out into a small cobblestone courtyard. I glanced around in the dim light. An old stone well sat at the center, overrun with vines and thick foliage. An iron fence surrounding the courtyard stood eight feet tall, covered in untrimmed bushes and sprawling ivy. But I could see the golden field beyond the fence.

I looked for an exit, a gate that would lead to freedom, but my search was cut short by whimpering.

Mournful, small cries that sounded like a hurt animal or maybe a scared child.

Carefully stepping across overgrowth and around bushes, I saw a body wrapped in thick ivy from shoulders to ankles. Another student faced away from me, bound and trapped in a hopeless predicament.

Without thinking, I dropped to the victim's side and tugged the body to face me, thinking it might be Mac or Boomer. I gasped and jumped back. It was Doris.

CHAPTER THIRTEEN

H er eyes were closed, her face pale, and her black hair tangled like a bird's nest. She moaned as her eyes fluttered open.

Her face tightened with a flash of rage. "Millie," she spat. She struggled against the vines and I scampered back a foot. The ivy tightened around Doris and her face twisted in pain. I could now see the thorns in those vines and understood her predicament.

Doris stilled, her breathing ragged, and she started to whimper again. What was I to do? She lifted desperate eyes to me. "Help me," she groaned.

Dean Kyra had said that our paths may cross and if they did we had permission to help one another. But we didn't have to. Doris had been nothing but unkind to me and my friends. If I were lying there and she came upon me, she'd surely laugh and walk away. I should do the same.

"Please," her small voice came again. "I'll die here if you leave me."

I knew Dean Kyra wouldn't let us die. But I also knew her pain was real. I wanted to walk away, but the anger and pride I'd felt a moment before began to fade. That wasn't the kind of person I was. And it wasn't who I wanted to be.

I approached Doris's side and knelt. "What happened?" I asked.

"I tried to cut through and they started attacking me," Doris said, glancing to her right. I followed her gaze and saw a small machete lying on the floor two paces away. Beside it lay a brick with an inscription. I quickly retrieved the brick and studied the inscription.

"Follow me to the source," I read aloud. "Hurry, I'm in need."

"I hate riddles," Doris whined.

"You didn't follow the rules," I scolded, once again tempted to leave her. "This is a mind challenge. You can't just hack your way out!" I glanced at the machete. "How'd you even get that blade?"

"How do you think?" she snarled.

She used her gift, I thought. *And it had failed her.*

"Get me out of these," Doris begged. "Cut me out!" She struggled again, unable to control herself. Again, the ivy tightened.

"Stop it!" I snapped. "The more you struggle, the more they tighten. You're only making it worse."

She inhaled and slowly relaxed. I watched the ivy loosen a bit but not enough to free her. We needed to solve the puzzle. I looked at the brick again. *Follow me to the source. Hurry, I'm in need.*

"Did you see a path anywhere?" I asked.

"No, and trust me, I searched," the bitter twin said.

I looked around. There was so much foliage, overgrown and covering much of the courtyard. Thick roots grew along the ground tangled with vines. An idea dropped into my mind. Maybe it wasn't a path we needed to follow but rather a root.

I jumped up.

"Please don't leave me," Doris whimpered.

I ignored her and traced the ivy that held her tight, following the vines down to her ankles and then back to the fence. "It's the roots," I said. "We have to follow the roots to their source."

I moved around Doris, doing my best not to touch the vines. Then I followed them along the fence toward the east side, leaving Doris behind. The roots snaked behind the well and toward the south wall near the passageway I'd escaped. There, behind an evergreen bush, I saw a collection of dying flowers. They slumped over toward the ground, gray and lifeless.

"Hurry, I'm in need," I whispered, repeating the second half of the riddle. They were dying and needed . . .

I spun around. "Water!" I rushed to the well and snatched up a half-buried wooden bucket. Raising it up, I dunked the bucket into the well water.

Doris started to scream, and I looked over my shoulder to see the ivy slowly pulling her toward the fence. *Like the walls closing in*, I thought. *Solve the riddle and things go from bad to worse.*

"Hold on!" I cried out.

In my rush to get back to the source of the vines, I spilled half the water. I dumped what remained over the flowers and waited a beat. Nothing happened. Maybe I needed more. Or maybe this wasn't the answer.

Hurrying back to the well, I refilled the bucket, this time moving toward the dying flowers with care to not spill. Doris's screams surrounded me as I splashed the water over the vines.

I took a breath. Nothing.

"Millie!" Doris yelled.

"Why isn't this working?" I demanded, starting to panic.

Maybe I was wrong. Why was the vine reacting so viciously?

I was at a loss, thinking maybe I should just take up the machete and try to cut Doris free when I saw the first twitch of life in the dead flowers and my heart went still. Right before my eyes, the gray flowers turned a brilliant blue and opened wide to the sky.

I'd done it. I'd solved the riddle!

The air had gone quiet. I spun back to Doris. The girl was pulling at the ivy, which had loosened its grip. She struggled to her feet, brushed her palms on her pants, and looked at me.

She was covered in small scrapes, and her shirt was darkened with spots of blood. Her hair was disheveled and her eyes drained. She looked weak, and for the first time I felt more powerful than her. I'd saved her. She'd needed me.

Maybe the potential Dean Kyra talked about *was* in me.

"You okay?" I asked.

"No," she said.

I knew I wasn't going to get a thank-you but I didn't need it. We both knew what had happened here.

"We still need to get out," she said.

"I think there's something over here," Doris said, crossing the courtyard. "It's what I was going for when the ivy attacked me."

She stopped in front of a thick wall of ivy. I made my way to her side and saw she was staring at something beyond the vines. Something that sparkled, as if made of gold. She glanced down at me and nodded toward it with her head.

She was afraid to touch the ivy after her last interaction with it. I exhaled nervously and stepped forward. Careful not to disturb too much, I gently parted the vines like a curtain.

Behind was a golden frame surrounding a picture of the very courtyard we were in.

"Help me," I said.

She hesitated but finally swallowed her fear and pulled back the rest of the ivy. We tucked it away from the painting and stared at the odd find. It stood over both our heads, wide and heavy. I ran my fingers across the art's surface. Canvas glued to wood.

"This is definitely out of place," I mumbled.

I looked back at Doris, who was undoubtedly having the same thought I was. To find the hidden stones, we were to look for something that didn't belong. Without having to say another word, both of us started examining the picture. I slid my fingers along the frame as she moved her hands across the painting.

"Here," she said a moment later, pulling at the bottom right corner. The canvas painting peeled away to reveal a small red cupboard two feet high and a foot wide. Doris reached forward and pulled the cupboard door open.

Inside was a single shelf and on it two items: a black orb and a white diamond. Doris reached in and yanked them both out.

We both stood, caught up in the moment, unsure what to do next.

"We each get one," I said, watching the wheels behind Doris's eyes work. She wanted them both. But so did I.

"I saved your life," I snapped. "You wouldn't have even found them if I hadn't freed you."

"And you wouldn't have found them if I hadn't been taken by the ivy."

"You don't know that. I've solved all the riddles in this challenge."

She thought about it, glanced at the items in her hands, and then held out the black orb. Without letting her reconsider, I snatched the item and clutched it close.

"We're even," Doris said. "And if you tell anyone you helped me, I'll make sure you regret it."

I hated the way fear crawled down my spine when she threatened me, and I tried hard to keep it from showing on my face. Before I could object, something creaked behind us and we turned to see that the painting was affixed to a gate, and the gate had popped open.

Doris pushed past me and yanked the gate wide. I quickly followed her through the opening into a large room filled with hay bales, open stalls, and empty troughs. Rafters held the roof in place.

A barn. I spun back. The courtyard had vanished.

The barn had several high windows near the roof but no doors that I could see, and no way to reach the windows.

"Find a way out," I said.

We began to search. It had to be like the other spaces. Another puzzle was hidden here somewhere. How many of these did I have to solve to be worthy of getting my gift? We each worked separately, searching every nook and cranny of the barn for at least five minutes.

A pungent scent filled my nostrils.

"You smell that?" I asked. "It's smells like . . ."

I saw the flames licking up the far corner of the barn, filling the air with thin smoke. I backed away as the flames spread. We were going to be burned alive!

"What do we do?" Doris cried.

"Use your gift!" I yelled.

The hay on the floor caught fire, and flames spread as if the floor had been doused in kerosene. I scrambled to get away as the fire crawled up the walls and licked at the ceiling. The beams crackled and popped as the flames' sharp teeth devoured them.

"Watch out!" Doris screamed. Two tumbled down toward us.

I launched myself away and landed hard. My head slammed on the ground, knocking me hard enough to see stars. I rolled to my stomach. I tried to stand up but my foot punched through the rotted floor.

My right leg crashed into the hole, all the way up to my knee, and I cried out as sharp shards of wood scratched the side of my calf.

Another beam crashed down, sending up an explosion of sparks. I tried yanking my leg out, but it wouldn't budge. My foot was stuck!

"Doris!" I cried, tugging with all my strength. Dark, heavy smoke roiled around me. I coughed as toxins filled my lungs.

"Doris!" I screamed, hacking violently.

She emerged from the smoke, her eyes wide as she looked down at me.

"Help me," I said, still pulling frantically to free my foot.

She stared for a moment, then glanced to my right. I followed her eyes to see that the black orb I'd stowed in my pocket sat on the floor just out of my reach. It must have fallen loose and rolled.

She swept up the orb and turned to leave me.

"Save me!" I screamed. "Please, you have to."

She looked back, a wicked look in her eyes. "We're even, remember."

Without another word she disappeared into the heavy smoke and heat. My eyes started to water. I cried out and pulled with everything I had, but my foot remained lodged.

Doris had betrayed me. I'd risked getting out of the house to help her, and she'd left me to burn. The fire inched closer and the heat of it stung my skin. I had been a fool and now I would pay for it.

I couldn't take air in without wheezing. Tears streamed from my eyes. My skin felt like it was blistering. And then everything went still and dark, and I knew I was being pulled from danger.

I was being rescued from death.

But not from failure.

CHAPTER FOURTEEN

It had been two days since the second challenge. Eleven more students had discovered their gifts in the puzzle house, including Boomer, who had a Nurture gift with a healer's ability. Even more had found a hidden stone to help them on the third and final challenge in the FIGS initiation trial. Only those who found their gift and completed the third and final challenge would be permitted to enter FIGS.

Two more students, Angela and Stanley, had decided to leave. The pain and fear of the trial were too much. Their departure meant only five students without gifts remained: one of the girls from my tent, Liana, who was the only girl smaller than me; a spacey kid named Logan, who didn't seem bothered; a boy named Sid, whom I'd never heard speak; Olive, who had escaped the house but without activating her gift; and me.

But the other four had found hidden stones. I was the only one without either a stone or a gift. I was the runt of the litter.

The other students whispered about me when they thought I wasn't listening. No one believed I was going to make it. Including me.

The days were long and the nights restless. My mind was full of dark thoughts concerning my failure to measure up and be accepted. To make matters worse, the nightmare of being betrayed by Doris replayed on a loop with the words that had accused me.

Something is wrong with you, Millie.

You're just a worthless girl.

You should be ashamed.

A hundred times I considered leaving. As I laid awake in bed. As I helped around camp. As I heard my friends express excitement about the ways their lives were changing. I hadn't been strong enough to complete the first challenge, and I'd been too foolish to succeed in the second, so what was the point of trying in the third?

I'd considered telling Mac and Boomer what had happened between Doris and me but knew there wasn't any point. Telling my friends would only confirm how stupid I'd really been. I guessed that Mac would have never helped Doris, and if she had, she certainly wouldn't have let Doris take both stones. That was my own fault.

The morning of the third day was warm. The sky was clear, filled with fluffy white clouds and singing blue birds. We'd finished breakfast—eggs, toast, bacon, and pineapple—and were walking to the main tent to get our chore assignments for the day.

We'd filled our days with work around the camp, doing our part as we waited anxiously for the third and final challenge. I often saw Mac staring at her palm and knew she was feeling her Nurturing power coursing under her skin. She'd catch me looking and quickly put her hand away.

"I can't wait till you get to feel this, Millie," she'd say.

I'd fake a smile in the awkward silence.

We'd almost reached the main tent when I glanced to my right to see Doris standing with a group ten yards off. We held eyes for a long second, anger and shame in equal measures gathering in my chest, then I tore my gaze from hers and turned back to my friends.

"What was that?" Mac asked. Boomer had noticed too and was looking at me suspiciously. Part of me wanted to tell the truth, but most of me didn't. I was embarrassed, and I could still feel Doris's eyes drilling a hole in my back.

I remembered her threat: *If you tell anyone you helped me . . .* I exhaled and shook my head, but before I could say anything, a cold voice cut through my thoughts.

"Well, well, well, if it isn't the gang of misfits." We all turned to see the Elite twins, followed by their clique of six bullies. Mac called them the goons.

"Go away, Dash," Mac said.

"What do misfits talk about when no one's listening?" Dash teased.

"Nothing worth repeating I would guess," Doris said, keeping her eyes on me.

She was warning me. I glared at her but didn't feel any courage.

She got in my face. "What are you looking at, Millie?"

"I should tell everyone," I whispered, my anger taking over my reason.

"Tell us what?" Mac asked close to my side.

Doris flicked her eyes to Mac, momentarily uneasy, but she quickly recovered and smirked. "Yes, please tell everyone about your second challenge experience. Tell us how you got your gift." Doris feigned a surprised face. "Oh wait, you can't. You didn't get a gift."

"Shut up, Doris," Mac snapped.

But Doris didn't shut up. "What about the hidden stones, Millie? Surely you found a stone, like everyone else!"

Behind her, the goons snickered and I felt my face flush.

"Yeah, Millie," Dash joined. "How does one come out of two challenges without a gift or a stone? Maybe your gift is to be worthless at everything."

"Shut up, Dash," Boomer defended.

Doris ignored him. "The challenges prove whether you're strong enough, smart enough, and good enough to be here. Guess what, Millie? Looks like you're not."

"Leave her alone," Mac said. "There's still one more challenge."

"Please," Dash said. "No one here actually believes she can succeed."

Mac's face darkened but she said nothing. Hopelessness filled my gut as my deepest fears were confirmed. Even my best friends doubted I would measure up. And why shouldn't they? I doubted myself too.

"You should just leave, Millie," Doris said. "Save yourself more embarrassment. Just go home. Surely someone somewhere wants you."

Tears blurred my vision.

"Oh no, Doris," Dash said, lifting his hand to his mouth. "You made little Millie cry."

"I . . . I . . ."

Shame smothered me. I couldn't find the right words.

"I . . . I . . . I . . . what?" Doris snapped. "Just give up. You don't belong here. We all know there's something wrong with you."

Her statement tore a hole through my heart like a bullet.

"You're just a misfit. Misfit Millie," Doris said.

"Yeah, Misfit Millie," Dash said with a crack of laughter. Their goons started to laugh as well, and Dash started to chant, "Misfit Millie, Misfit Millie, Misfit Millie!"

I couldn't handle it anymore. I pushed past the group and rushed toward the edge of camp. Mac called after me, but I ignored her as Doris and her lackeys' laughter chased me.

I ran past Dean Kyra's tent and out into the grassy field, then continued into the trees until the sounds of their cruelty faded. My heart ached and a lump filled my throat when I finally slowed and fell to my knees at the base of a large pine tree.

I cried until my chest hurt. Cried because they were right. Everyone was right. I didn't belong here. Something was wrong with me. Even the woodsman had warned me, but I'd been too stupid to listen, and now everyone knew how weak I really was.

I wanted to go home, even though I didn't know where or what home was. I found myself thinking about what Peter said: it had to be better than this.

A twig snapped and I jerked my head toward the sound. The woodsman appeared from the cover of the trees, his face somber. Without a word, he reached out his hand to help me up. I sniffed back my tears and swallowed hard as I accepted his offer. He pulled me to my feet, and for a moment we just stood there as he searched my eyes.

He is the only one who really understands me, I thought. *A truth teller who has my best interests in mind.*

The woodsman placed a soft hand on my shoulder. Tears rolled down my cheeks and I dropped my head. The woodsman pulled me into his large frame and my forehead fell against his chest. I wept long and hard as the grizzly man gently held me.

My crying finally settled and he stepped back. I wiped my nose with the back of my hand and brushed tears from my cheeks.

"You were right," I sniffed. "My dream was a warning."

"Dreams often are," the woodsman said.

"I should have listened. Now everyone knows what a failure I am."

"Accepting what you are doesn't make you a failure. It makes you wise, Millie."

"I'm a failure who doesn't deserve a medallion."

The woodsman huffed and shook his head. "Why do you want a medallion so badly anyway?"

"Because . . ." I started, but then I couldn't think of a good answer.

"Because you believe the lie that getting a medallion will make you powerful. What they don't tell you is that it's all a trap. A way to get you to buy into false ideas about who you are."

He crossed his arms.

"Why do you think they take your memories?"

It was a good question. Dean Kyra said it was so we could see beyond the limitations of our histories.

"So they can cut you off from who you really are," the woodsman said. "But you're like me, Millie. You can hear the truth inside. Your instincts are telling you to leave this place because it isn't safe. Because you don't belong here."

Pain stabbed at my chest.

"You think that's a bad thing, but maybe your wisdom, the part of you that knows you best, is trying to spare you from the greater pain coming," he continued. "You're the lucky one, Millie. I wasn't as lucky."

"You were like me?" I asked.

"A long time ago," he said. "I only wish I'd had someone to help me see through their dangerous game."

"What happened?"

He sighed and shook his head. "I lost everything, and what I got in return wasn't worth it. That's why I don't use my gift anymore. It's also why I remain here, living off the forest. Here, I can help those wise enough to listen."

"Does Dean Kyra know?"

"Of course. She knows that the wisest will listen, and that's perfectly fine with her. She has a good heart. She knows my way is the quickest way through FIGS, right past all the madness and back to freedom."

It made a kind of strange sense to me. Maybe I was being the wisest of them all. Maybe my gift was listening to what no one else was willing to hear.

"Have you told others?" I asked.

"The others don't see with clear eyes like you do. Few do. They're blinded by their own disbelief. They'll have to learn the hard way." He took a step toward me and dropped his voice. "But you know the truth, Millie. Stop running from it."

He tucked my hair behind my ear and gave my shoulder a soft squeeze. "Save yourself before it's too late."

Fear galloped like a horse across my heart. "How?"

"Listen carefully to the voice of warning," he said. "What's it telling you to do?"

I didn't have to think hard.

Something is wrong with you, Millie. You don't belong here. You're just a foolish, worthless girl.

The woodsman held my eyes as tears slipped down my cheeks. The voices were cruel, but they felt truer than anything else I knew.

As if reading my mind, the woodsman said, "Sometimes the truth can be hard to hear, but if you follow it, it will keep you safe."

I believed him. He may have been the only person who'd been honest with me from the start, and he was right. I'd known all along that I didn't belong here. I didn't even want to be here. Peter and the others who'd left had it right. This place wasn't safe.

I wanted to leave.

I was done with it all.

CHAPTER FIFTEEN

I left the woodsman, feeling both relieved and saddened. Relieved because I had finally decided to listen to the voice that was telling me to leave, but sad because it meant saying good-bye to my new friends. I hoped I had friends like them back in my old life. I had to, right? Everyone had friends.

Camp was nearly empty. The students must have been off gathering wood and doing other chores. A couple Leads were standing on a hill. The teachers were likely in their tents.

I was headed for Dean Kyra's tent when Professor Gabriel stepped out of a tent to my right, whistling a happy tune.

"Millie Maven," he said, delighted. "What a pleasant surprise."

"Hello, Professor Gabriel."

He pulled up, studying my face. "Something is wrong?"

I hesitated. "Do you know if Dean Kyra's in her tent?"

"I'm not sure. Can I ask why?"

"I need to speak with her right away."

"Oh," he said, pushing his wire-rimmed glasses up the bridge of his nose. "Sounds very important indeed."

"It is," I said.

"Give me a moment and I'll check for you." He stepped into Dean Kyra's tent and returned alone a few moments later. "So sorry, dear. She must be with other students. You'll have to wait."

I couldn't wait. With each passing moment I was more certain I had to get out of here.

"Maybe I can help?" Professor Gabriel said.

I was ashamed to say it, but I was more afraid to stay.

"I want to go home." My voice was small under the weight of my misery.

"I see," Professor Gabriel said, his face gentle. "And why is that?"

"I don't belong here. I've known it from the start. My place is home. That's my gift. That's what I came to learn, that nothing except home is where I belong, so I need to go back."

Professor Gabriel was quiet for a moment. "Can I show you something?" he asked.

"What? I want to go—"

"Yes, home, and that is your choice to make, of course. I will escort you to the shore myself, but would you humor an old teacher and allow me to take you one place first? It would be a shame to leave without seeing it."

I sniffed back my tears and gave a heavy sigh. "Okay."

"Excellent," he said and clapped his hands together once. "Follow me."

He turned and headed for his tent, second down the row from Dean Kyra's. I followed him inside. It was nothing special, holding a couple worktables filled with papers and books, along with some reading shelves and cushioned chairs. He walked straight to the back of the tent, parted two flaps, and exited. I followed on his heels.

The moment I stepped outside, I gasped. I'd expected to see woods, thick with trees, the sky hidden by foliage. Instead I was surrounded by a lush garden. Brightly colored flowers grew in bunches everywhere, and rows of tall, manicured rosebushes in full bloom lined either side of a path that stretched before me. Light-green trees with weeping boughs that bent nearly to the ground replaced the dark forest pines. Others with bushy tops flowered with tiny white buds.

I looked at Professor Gabriel in wonder and he gave me a wink, motioning me to follow. The blossoming flowers were of innumerable shapes, sizes, and colors. Brilliant yellows and oranges. Deep purples and blues. Pristine whites, stunning reds. I'd never seen a place like this before, a wide garden, perfectly kept, warm, and peaceful. The sorrow and pain that had filled me only a moment before started to fade, replaced with amazement.

"Where are we?" I asked.

"The campus garden," Professor Gabriel said. "One of my favorite places to reflect." We rounded a hedge and I saw a round stone fountain. Its water shimmered in shades of blue and green, and sunlight sparkled on the surface like a layer of diamonds. The sight trans-fixed me.

"I thought a tour of the grounds would be of help," Gabriel said. He added something else, but my mind was on the water.

I touched the water with my fingertips. It was warm and familiar though I couldn't place why. Did I know this water?

"Well, hello, my dear," a voice said ahead of me.

I looked up and saw a beautiful woman of average height and build with soft brown hair and matching eyes. Her round face and light-pink cheeks held a wide welcoming smile as warm as the water lingering on my fingers. She wore simple clothes and a wide-brimmed sunhat, green garden gloves, and tall black rubber boots.

"My name is Rebecca," the woman said. "And who are you?"

I glanced back to take direction from Professor Gabriel, but he was gone. He'd left me? The thought gave me a beat of fear, but then the woman's appearance and gentle voice warmed my heart.

"Millie Maven," I said.

"You're one of the new students," Rebecca said.

"Yes," I replied. "Are you a teacher?"

"Heavens no. I tend the gardens at FIGS. Rain or shine you can always find me here."

She was younger than any of the teachers I'd met but old enough to be a mother to any of us. Something about that was strangely alluring. As though she might offer to take me home, cook me a hot meal, tuck me in, and watch over me until I fell asleep.

Rebecca the motherly gardener stepped up to me. As she did, a small blue bird plopped down on her shoulder and tweeted a sharp note into her ear.

She didn't look worried at all.

"Yes, yes," she said, as the bird tweeted again. "This is Paxaro, watcher of the garden." The bird hopped up into the air and in a single swoosh landed on my shoulder. I flinched and Rebecca chuckled.

"He has a problem with minding personal space," Rebecca said. "Here, extend your arm like this." She lifted my arm and the blue bird jumped down to perch on my forearm.

I looked at the small creature as it surveyed me, tilting its head back and forth in quick movements. He chirped at me, and it made me smile. "Hello, Paxaro."

"It means 'bird' in Galician," Rebecca said. "He named himself."

"He named himself?"

"But of course."

Maybe birds could talk here. Or maybe Rebecca just knew how to interpret their songs.

Paxaro launched from my arm and took to the sky, singing to other birds, which responded in kind as he went. Was that bird talk?

"So, what brings you into my neck of the woods?" Rebecca asked.

"I . . ." There was still no sign of the professor, but

I didn't feel afraid. "Professor Gabriel said something about a tour."

"Well, we can definitely do that," Rebecca said, eyes bright. "I would never turn down the opportunity to share beauty with someone as beautiful as you."

She thought I was beautiful? No one had ever said such a thing, not that I could remember, and I'd never seen such a beautiful place. Besides, Rebecca smelled like lavender and pollen, a strong combination that I liked very much.

"Okay," I said.

A commanding chirp sounded overhead as another blue bird soared across the sky with Paxaro.

"Shall we?" Rebecca asked.

I walked with Rebecca, feeling oddly at ease and full of wonder. She showed me the garden with pride, her voice warm and her excitement contagious. She spoke about each plant we passed as though it was the most beautiful thing in the garden, and I believed her. But not everything could be the most beautiful; that wasn't the way the world worked. Still, Rebecca made me think maybe it could.

The garden stretched beyond my view in each direction, filled with every kind of flower and plant a person could imagine, plus some I'm pretty sure couldn't be imagined. Groves of trees towered into the sky and swayed with the breeze. All different kinds with different colored bark, some filled with fruit, others home to small squirrels and colorful birds. Rabbits and chipmunks and other small creatures I didn't recognize popped up here and there, curious about our passing.

There were stone benches for sitting and gazing, as well as a small stone bridge that crossed a stream. The water in the stream was the same as the water in the fountain. Brilliant-orange fish jumped out of the water to greet us as we passed.

Paxaro frequently swooped down to sing to us, and I laughed as Rebecca interpreted the bird's crazy antics. I lost myself in the moment, the fear of failing FIGS only a pinprick thought hidden behind the joy of being with the garden keeper and her bird.

After completing the tour, Rebecca led me back to the fountain where we'd started. She sat on the stone edge and patted the flat surface next to her. I hopped up and for a moment we sat in silence, content to listen to the sounds of the gurgling water and chirping birds.

"It's magnificent," Rebecca said. "Don't you think?"

"Magnificent," I said. "You did all this?"

She chuckled. "No, no. This is the Great Teacher's garden; I only tend it."

"People keep talking about him, but I still

don't know who he is."

"He's beyond all names," Rebecca said with a twinkle in her eyes. "A creator, an artist, a father, a son, a friend, but mostly he is what his name suggests: the truth itself, and certainly the greatest teacher any could possibly encounter."

The thought of meeting him excited me. "Will I get to meet him?"

She tilted her head slightly. "I thought you were leaving."

Her question reminded me of my trouble. I dropped my eyes to my feet and nodded. "Yeah."

"I'm sorry to hear that," Rebecca said. "He would have loved to have spent time with you."

"I doubt that," I said.

"You seem so sure."

"I don't belong here with medallions and grand gardens and Great Teachers."

"Why not?"

"Because I know who I am. I know my limitations." I paused, thinking about the voice of reason that had warned me. "I've always known."

"And who do you think you are, Millie Maven?" Rebecca asked.

I shivered as a knot of shame formed in my throat.

I was tired of crying, my chest sore from heaving. I wanted to be able to tell this beautiful stranger that I was strong, brave, smart—a girl worthy of power, but that would all be a lie.

"I'm worthless," I said, holding back tears.

"Who told you that?" Rebecca asked.

"No one had to tell me; it's just the truth. I can feel it inside." I hopped down off the fountain edge, tears escaping my eyes. I felt embarrassed and didn't want Rebecca to see me cry. "I don't expect anyone to understand."

"I do, though," Rebecca said. "I've felt worthless plenty. At times, I still do."

I faced her, taken aback. "You?"

"Of course. Having emotions is only human. But then I remember something very important, and my feelings of worthlessness are soon swept away." She slid off the fountain and continued. "I'm not worthless."

The simple remark struck me deeply.

"I can show you if you want," Rebecca said, holding out her hand for me to take.

CHAPTER SIXTEEN

I thought against it, but something about the garden keeper drew me in. My heart trusted her, even as my mind warned against her tricks. I took her hand and we walked past the fountain, through a collection of orange trees, down a small dirt path lined with lilacs, and to the edge of the stream.

"The water in this place isn't just any water," Rebecca said. "It's mysterious and works in ways only the Great Teacher fully understands. It holds great power for restoration and healing. But more, it opens the mind to the Great Teacher so that his truth can be heard."

Rebecca paused and a shadow of sorrow crossed her face. "Many have forgotten his truth. They've forgotten the way that he came to show. His life, death, and resurrection point to a whole new way of being. It was he who said that unless a seed falls to the ground and dies, it cannot bear new fruit. He showed the way. He is the way."

She turned to me and placed her hands on my shoulders. "If you want to hear what he thinks about you, all you have to do is drink." She left me standing alone at the stream's edge.

I glanced at the water, the blue-green color sparkling, waves of light flowing beneath the surface. It almost felt as though the water was speaking to me—not audibly, but as a feeling deep in my gut urging me to drink.

I knelt and cupped water into the palms of my hands. It was warm and held a slight charge that prickled my skin. I felt a beat of fear, but the water was too compelling, and without another thought I pressed my hands to my lips and drank.

Although warm against my palms, it was cool over my tongue and down my throat, refreshing and soothing, as though I'd been dying of thirst. With one small sip, my thirst was quenched. I closed my eyes at the taste and smell. Sweet like fresh fruit and honey. Fragrant like spring rain and lilies. But mostly what I felt was power as the energy of that water filled my belly and spread throughout my body.

I snapped open my eyes and saw nothing had changed. I'd expected something to be different. Maybe the water hadn't worked. I turned to ask Rebecca, but she was gone. She'd abandoned me too?

Paxaro swooped down from the sky and perched on the ground a few feet in front of me. He chirped, twitching his head back and forth, then began to hop toward the stone bridge behind me. I watched him hop to the middle of the bridge, where he stopped and looked back at me.

He chirped a couple times, as if calling to me. *He wants me to follow*, I thought. A small smile crept over my lips. *Were birds even capable of such things? I wondered.* But after more persistent chirping, I followed. Across the bridge and then down a small path into another section of the garden as colorful and lush as the rest.

Paxaro hopped along, occasionally taking to the air to fly a couple feet and then landing to hop more. Where was he leading me? We traveled for a few minutes until we came to a massive willow tree in a small clearing. It had to be as big as any mansion or castle, and its leafy branches hung all the way to the grass, so thick I couldn't see through them. I'd never seen a tree so large.

Paxaro gave a final tweet and then hopped in through the weeping willow's branches. I took a deep breath and did the same, slowly parting the leaves with my hands and stepping through.

I looked around to see a near perfect circle surrounded completely by the willow's drooping foliage. Inside the canopy, white lilies grew in bunches from the grass around the willow's large trunk. Vines with white blossoms accented the branches.

To the left of the large tree sat a simple wooden bench.

Millie.

I gasped and turned, looking for a source. There was no one, naturally, because the voice was coming from within me. I knew that, but it had sounded so real! I was alone in the place, but not alone, because now there was a voice in me.

Millie, sit with me.

My heart leaped, drawn by that gentle voice. I immediately knew this was the Great Teacher. Not in body but in spirit, filling my mind and my heart. How I knew, I couldn't say, but that voice cannot be mistaken by any, ever.

Sit and let me tell you the ways I love you.

My mind froze. *It is a cruel trick*, I thought, *because no one really loves me.* A part of me said it was a mocking voice.

My mind froze, but my heart was opened wide by that powerful voice.

I love you. Sit with me and I will tell you.

My feet moved before my mind could object any further. I walked to the wooden bench and eased to my seat, heart now racing.

All sound fell away the moment I sat. In that silent space, the air itself seemed to be alive, thriving with power. Something important was about to happen. When the voice spoke again, it was as though every cell of my body reacted to the power of each syllable.

I love you more than a flower loves the rain, or a tree loves the sun.

I love you more than a mother and father care for their only child.

I love you more than the light of a million stars.

Silent tears were streaming down my cheeks. My heart desperately wanted to believe the voice, but my mind still objected. I didn't know why, because I didn't know who I'd been before coming to FIGS. But apparently I hated myself.

I called you to this place so you could see who you are and how much you are loved.

"You wouldn't love me if you knew me," I whispered.

I do know you. I'm the one who called you for a very special reason.

The words were too much to bear. Guilt for not being good enough swarmed me.

"It can't be me," I said past a knot in my throat. "I'm not special."

It has always been you. You are the one I chose.

"But I'm not strong." My voice was so weak the words hardly left my mouth. I could taste salty tears on my lips.

You were strong enough to dive into a pool when called.

I had no memory of that, but maybe it was true.

"But I'm foolish," I objected still.

You were wise enough to help another despite being enemies.

"I don't belong here. Something is wrong with me."

Don't listen to the lies of fear. Instead hear my voice: You, Millie Maven, I call mine. Chosen and set on a path to experience my love in you. When the master of deception comes, listen only to what I say about you. I call you perfect, whole, washed clean by my death and life of all that blinds you to the truth.

My whole body trembled. The power of those words washed over me like waves, promising to cleanse me of the shame and fear I'd brought to FIGS from a distant land. Hope flooded me, but could I really trust?

I call you mine.

I wanted to believe. I desperately wanted to believe every beautiful word.

With a deep exhale, I released the last of my reservations and I did believe. A small blossom of joy exploded into a heatwave of peace that crashed over me, and for the first time that I could remember I felt worthy. Welcomed. Loved.

I sat on that bench for a while, soaking in the presence of a truth I'd never known. A truth I didn't want to forget. I was afraid to leave, afraid the second I left the protection of the willow I'd realize it was all a trick of my mind.

Now go, Millie Maven, and finish what I called you to. Don't be afraid. I am with you always.

The voice flooded my chest and I smiled. I didn't know what was going to happen when I returned to camp, and I was still unnerved by it all, but for the first time I felt worthy of the journey.

I would do what the Great Teacher had asked.

I would return to camp and I would finish.

I didn't see Rebecca as Paxaro led me out of the garden. New questions began popping into my mind. Questions like, how can I be sure that was the voice of the Great Teacher? How do I know I can trust it? What if it was just trying to trick me into staying? But as quickly as the questions came, echoes of the Great Teacher's voice snuffed them out.

The sky was turning from dusk to dark when I

reached a lone tent at the edge of the garden and Paxaro flew away. *This must be the tent through which I'd entered*, I guessed. So I parted the flaps at the back, walked through the large canvas tent, and stepped out the other side.

Fires were being lit as people moved about, but no one seemed to notice me.

Students were exiting the mess tent, and I wondered if I'd missed dinner. As I walked across the grassy middle path, I felt eyes and turned to see Professor Gabriel smiling at me. I returned the gesture and he gave me a small nod. I started making my way toward him when Dash, Doris, and their gang exited the mess tent.

They spotted me and whistled.

"Well, well," Dash said. "Thought maybe you took our advice and left since we didn't see you at dinner."

I didn't want to engage them. I didn't want to fall back into their trap. I was thankful to see Mac push her way through the twins toward me. Boomer was right behind.

"Millie!" Mac cried. "I've been looking everywhere for you."

"We," Boomer corrected. "*We* have been looking."

Mac looped her arm through mine and pulled me

away as Boomer tagged along. Doris said something, but Mac just turned her head and yelled, "Leave it alone, Doris!"

I smiled as the three of us separated ourselves from the others. Once alone, Mac turned to me, tears misting her eyes. "Millie, I am so sorry."

"About what?" I asked.

"When Doris asked if I believed you would get your gift, I should have said something. I would totally understand if you hate me."

"We both should have," Boomer said. "We're really sorry."

"Of course we think you're going to get your gift. I mean, I don't even want to be here if you aren't," Mac said.

"It's okay," I said, jumping in while Mac took a breath. "Really, guys, I don't hate you. It's okay."

"Really?" Mac said, the worry easing from her face. "I was so worried." She yanked me into a hug that was too tight, and Boomer collapsed his arms around us both. I chuckled and struggled to breathe but welcomed the affection.

Mac pulled back and exhaled. "Where have you been?"

I looked to make sure no one else was around.

"Something happened to me," I said. "Something unbelievable."

"What?" Mac asked.

I swallowed, afraid of what might happen if I told them. Would they believe me? Would it change things? They both stared at me, waiting.

"I think I met the Great Teacher," I said, keeping my voice low, close to a whisper.

"Like, you saw him?" Mac asked.

"No, I heard him," I said. "It's kind of hard to explain."

Mac and Boomer shared a strange, confused look that made me regret saying anything. "What is it?" I asked.

"We've heard Chaplin and Riggs talking about him a couple times, and rumor is no one has seen or heard from him in a long time. There was a time when he was around, but he disappeared. Some even think he was never real."

I shook my head. "No, he's real." *He must be*, I thought. Then I had an idea. "I can show you."

I started back toward the tent, Mac and Boomer following, careful to avoid prying eyes. Satisfied we were unseen, I led them inside, happy to see it was empty. "This way," I whispered over my shoulder as I hurried to the back of the tent. I pushed through the back flaps and gasped.

"What?" Boomer asked.

There was no garden, only forest and meadow. The same that wrapped around camp, the same that had always been here.

"I . . . I . . ." I stumbled.

"What's wrong?" Mac asked.

"It was here," I said, frantically looking around. "It was right here, a garden. Only a few minutes ago. That's where I met him. How could it not be here?"

"Maybe it was a dream?" Boomer asked carefully.

I spun toward them. "It wasn't! It was real."

"It's okay, Millie," Mac said, stepping forward and taking my hand. "We believe you."

But I could see the doubt in her eyes. A terrible thought dropped into my head: What if it hadn't been real?

CHAPTER SEVENTEEN

A loud, familiar bell gonged out across the night sky, three large clangs that could only mean one thing: it was time for the third challenge.

I walked with Mac and Boomer back to the center of camp as the remaining students came from all corners, gathering before Dean Kyra, who stood illuminated by the glow of the fires. The Leads and professors flanked her.

"We started with twenty-four students," Dean Kyra began. "We've lost some along the way, which is unfortunate but expected. Of this remaining group, sixteen of you have your medallions. You should be proud. As I said on the first day we met, I knew this group would be strong."

I avoided eye contact with anyone as an all too

familiar dread crept up my spine. Just like that, the calm and courage I'd felt in the garden were gone.

"Only five of you have yet to unlock your gifts. The third and final challenge will be your last opportunity to qualify for FIGS. It will be the most difficult challenge you have yet faced, requiring your physical fortitude, your mind, and the full strength of your heart."

She paused to let her words sink in, then continued. "Some of you have found the hidden stones that can assist you throughout this next challenge. It will be up to you to decipher how they are used. I will say this: one will guide you, and the other defend you."

A riddle. The students started to whisper. I felt dizzy, knowing I would face the most trying of the challenges without any help. I tried listening for the voice again, hoping its peace would emerge, but all I found was the slamming of my heart. Again, the terrifying question echoed through my brain: *What if it wasn't real?*

The scene around us began to change. The tents faded, the fires snuffed out, even the woods vanished, leaving us in a vast desert.

Mac clasped my hand and Boomer edged in closer as we surveyed the new surroundings. It was still dark, the night sky filled with brilliant stars and a bright round moon. We stood as a group, facing the only anomaly in that desert.

A green hedge, thick and massive as a wall, stood twenty paces away. It was at least a hundred feet tall and had to be hundreds of yards wide. A single door stood directly in front of us. Torches were planted along the hedge every dozen yards, their flames casting shadows that danced across the leaves.

Dean Kyra motioned to the monstrosity behind her.

"This is the grand maze, where your final challenge will take place. You will enter as a group, but finding your way through is your journey alone. The only rule is simple: you must find the exit. There are no short-cuts."

She stepped aside and faced the looming wall, a dark-green monstrosity on desert sand. "Make it through using your gifts and the hidden stones wisely, and you will have completed your Initiation Trial and qualified for entrance into FIGS. As always, may the Great Teacher guide you."

With that she stepped aside and swept her hand toward the looming maze.

We started forward as a group, following the twins, who barged ahead. The sheer size of the maze unnerved me. Up close, the top of the towering hedge was barely visible against the dark night sky. Through the entrance, we were met with more of the same: dense, towering walls of brush so thick they might as well be made of stone.

Seeing Doris turn to the left, I turned to my right with Mac and Boomer and started walking. The farther we got from the entry, the darker it became. Others followed, all of us moving carefully, unsure of what was coming.

The sound of breaking branches and rustling leaves drew everyone's attention back the way we'd come. The hedges were growing toward one another to seal up the place we had just entered!

My pulse spiked. Several gasped in the darkness. We were trapped.

"Should have left when you could, Millie Misfit," Doris said to my right. She and Dash must have cut back and followed us. "Too late now." And with that the twins took off down a narrow passage. All but Mac and Boomer followed them, emboldened by their confidence.

Mac watched them go, shaking her head. "I hope those two get eaten by a plant," she whispered.

"You think there will be flesh-eating plants?" Boomer squeaked out.

"Let's stick together as long as we can," Mac said.

Boomer and I nodded. We came to a three-way intersection: right, left, or straight down the center. Nothing distinguished one path from another. I was certain all three were dangerous.

"This way," Mac said, pointing to the right.

I nodded, glad to have Mac taking the lead. Boomer and I followed her. The narrow passage zigged then zagged, right then left, then right again. We encountered another intersection and decided to go left. Then another and we went right.

After only four turns, we reached a dead end. There was nothing to do but return to an intersection. We retraced our steps and went the opposite direction. A few minutes later we found ourselves at another dead end.

Boomer huffed. "Should've let me lead."

"You're welcome to reveal all your knowledge about this maze at any point," Mac snapped.

I heard something rustling to my right about four feet away.

"We should've at least stuck with the other people," Boomer continued. "Now we're totally lost."

I stepped forward to get a closer look. Tiny popping sounds were joined by small white buds pushing through the hedge. The flowers were strangely beautiful in the moonlight as they began to bloom. But something felt off.

"Hey, guys?" I said.

"You can help too, you know," Mac snapped at me. "I just . . ." Then she saw the budding flowers and swallowed her words. "What's happening?"

Mesmerized, I watched as the buds continued to bloom into open flowers. The centers were red, dotted with tiny sharp teeth. One sprang off the brush with a hiss and I reacted too late. It attached itself to my forearm. A hundred tiny daggers dug into my skin. I yelped and jumped back, ripping the thing off my arm.

Boomer and Mac rushed over as the flower fell from my arm, landed on the ground, and dissolved to dust.

"What is that?" Boomer asked.

Fresh blood soaked through my shirt sleeve; my arm throbbed. More popping interrupted any answer I could have given as all of us looked up and saw that the hedge was hatching hundreds of white buds, all of them blooming for attack.

"Oh man," Mac whispered, facing the other direction. Both hedge walls were filling with the little white monsters.

"Flesh-eating plants," Boomer whimpered.

"Run!" I shouted.

Something hissed past my left ear. We ran as fast as we could, tiny white flower monsters lunging from the walls, hungry for a bite of our flesh. Then there were hundreds, maybe thousands, hurtling through the air, their pops and hisses now deafening.

Mac cried out as one latched onto her shoulder and another onto her bicep. I pumped my legs faster, leading Mac and Boomer just ahead of the wave. I could hear the little monsters hissing and popping right behind us as we tore down the passage. Several reached me and I madly smacked them away as I ran.

"Go, go, go!" Boomer yelled, streaking past me. We rounded the next corner expecting to see the intersection we'd last taken. Boomer slid to a full stop and Mac nearly crashed into him.

Where only minutes earlier there had been an intersection, now there was only hedge. A dead end!

We searched frantically for a way out.

"There's nothing!" Boomer yelled.

I spun back around, frozen by the sight of thousands of flowers budding on the walls, popping open, getting ready to strike.

Mac jumped in front of us, turned to the growing army, and raised her right hand. The entire scene went still. Every flower, whether popping, budding, or flying, froze in place.

I gasped. Mac was holding them back. She was using her gift, her free hand wrapped around her medallion. I could see her arms shaking and hear her labored breathing.

"I don't know if I can hold them long," she said through gritted teeth.

"There has to be a way out," I cried, tugging at Boomer, who was staring like a statue. I madly shoved my hands into the hedge, searching for any escape. Boomer just stood behind me, transfixed.

"Boomer!" I shouted. "Help me!"

"Hurry!" Mac said. She was losing hold. I could see some flowers twitching in the air as others started to move in slow motion.

"One will guide you," Boomer mumbled.

"Boomer!" I yelled.

"The orb," he said, yanking it from his pocket. He looked it over, still doing nothing, as I frantically looked for a way to save us. I would have thrown a rock at him if I could have found one, and just as I was about to tell him so, he threw the small black orb against the ground as hard as he could.

With a loud thump, the orb shattered. Brilliant light filled the sealed hedge, and I threw my arm up to shield my eyes. Within a moment, the light faded to a normal glow.

The riddle! Of course! *One will guide you.* A light.

But it was a special light, because it revealed a three-foot hole in the wall. Maybe it created that hole. Either way, it was there now, and the orb was guiding us toward it.

Boomer saw it too.

"Mac! We found a way out!" I said. "Right wall, bottom left corner."

"You two go first," Mac said. "I'm right behind you."

Boomer didn't have to be told twice. He dropped and crawled through. Mac was backing up toward me as I dropped to do the same.

"Mac," I said, not wanting to leave her.

"Go, Millie!"

I crawled through. It wasn't very long, and I could feel branches scraping against my back. I had just exited the other side when I heard the hissing start again. Mac was right behind me, pulling herself out of the hole. She rolled, turned toward the hole, and with whatever strength she had left, sealed the small space behind us.

On the other side, the hissing rose to a crescendo as the monsters converged on the sealed passage. We sat there huffing, aching, Mac dripping in sweat.

"You okay?" I asked her.

"I think so," she breathed.

"We should keep going," Boomer said, helping Mac to her feet.

I pushed myself up and looked around. We were still in the maze but in another passage. This one was much wider, with a stone fountain up ahead. It reminded me of the garden. Assuming the garden had even been real.

The fountain rose from wide flagstones that formed a perfect square, ten feet to a side. Hedges met the square floor at each corner, revealing four paths that jutted from the fountain. A four-way intersection.

Somewhere in the distance, a high-pitched howl flowed across the sky.

"Flesh-eating plants and wolves," Boomer said. "I hate this maze."

Mac stepped onto the stone floor and walked up to the fountain, her boots clicking as she moved. "There's no water in it."

"Wonder why it's here," I said, joining her.

"Anyone got a penny?" Boomer asked, staring down into the empty basin. "Maybe we could wish ourselves out of here."

"The only way out is through," Mac said.

"It was a joke."

Mac cast him a glance. "Yeah, a bad joke."

I was going to tell them both to stop when the ground under us started to rumble. The vibration was gentle at first, but with each passing second it grew. I grasped the edge of the fountain for support. To our left, a flagstone broke with a loud crack. The break spread in a zigzag line across the floor.

Another crack echoed to the right, the report knocking me to my backside as more crooked cracks formed under my feet. The ground was breaking apart!

"Get off the floor!" Mac yelled. She was trying to help me up when she let out a yelp and was jerked away. I twisted to see a thick vine wrapped around her ankle, pulling her.

"Mac!"

I managed to push myself up as the floor continued to shake. But it was no use because the earthquake worsened and sharp boulders started jutting up through the ground, knocking me backward. I fell hard against the cracked ground and felt it give way under my weight. My fall into the open ground was only a few feet, but my hard landing knocked the wind from me.

Sucking at the air, I turned to my stomach and pushed up to my knees.

"Boomer?" I gasped.

Nothing

"Mac!"

No one replied. I could see the broken fountain above me and knew I could reach it by crawling up the stone slabs that had fallen into the ground with me. I reached the surface and scrabbled toward the fountain. But I had moved only three feet when a vine wrapped around my ankle tightly. It yanked me back to the ground and started pulling we away.

Screaming in rage now, I used my free foot to kick at my attacker. It was strong and fast. My back scraped against the uneven ground. I had to anchor myself!

I managed to get my hands on a thick piece of stone, but it popped free from the ground and came away in my hand. I could use it as a weapon.

The ground turned to dirt and grass as the vine yanked me from the flagstones onto another path. I lifted the stone and then slammed it down onto the vine with all my might.

The vine screamed, a shrill sound that hurt my ears. I pounded it again, then again, and it finally loosened its grip. After my final blow, the vine let go and slithered back into the darkness.

I dropped the stone, scrambled to my feet and tore back toward where I thought the fountain must be.

But the hedges were growing together again, this time cutting me off from Mac and Boomer.

"Mac!" I screamed as I raced toward the hedge.

But it was too late. I slammed into the sealed hedge with an angry cry. I'd lost them. The quaking had subsided. The night air was still.

I turned to face the dark maze, which was alive in every way.

I was inside of a monster, and I was alone.

Chapter Eighteen

I called for Mac and Boomer over and over. They didn't respond. My mind spun through the horrifying possibilities of what could have befallen them and I felt sick. I couldn't get lost in those thoughts, so I pushed them all down deep into my gut. The only choice was to move onward. The bright moon helped shed light on the path as I headed deeper into the maze, utterly lost. The path through the tall hedges led me left, then right, leaving me no options other than forward or back. But there was no going back for me.

I had walked maybe three minutes when a branch snapped behind me. I caught my breath and looked around, scanning the dark for the source of the noise. I couldn't see anything.

I exhaled and continued, picking up my pace. Another turn and another, down the empty path with towering hedges. Again I heard something—this time a shuffle—and again I whipped around, searching the darkness. I was about to head on when a low, deep growl rooted me to the ground.

Wolves.

My heart seized and my skin went cold. I slowly backed away as a set of deadly red eyes emerged from around a corner. A moment later the first set of eyes was joined by two more. They were following me and closing in, growling as they stalked me.

My instincts kicked in and I started running. A shrill howl echoed through the night behind me and I knew they were in pursuit. A glance over my shoulder showed them trotting as if in no hurry. As if they knew I couldn't escape them. As if they had hunted this way a hundred times and already accepted their inevitable victory.

I raced as fast as I could around another corner, nearly toppling over as my right shoulder clipped the hedge. Righting myself, I pushed harder, doing my best to ignore the accusing voices that insisted I had no hope.

I was just a girl and they were wolves.

I had nothing to defend myself and nowhere to hide.

I was dead meat.

Their growls grew as they steadily closed the distance. Tearing around another corner, I saw the dim outline of a fork in the path. I didn't have time to think about options, so I just picked a path and veered to the left.

But I quickly feared I'd made the wrong choice, because the hedges on either side narrowed almost immediately. The farther I ran, the slimmer the path became. Panic swallowed me. Was this the wolves' strategy? They knew I was coming to a dead end.

The hedges scraped my shoulders as I pushed ahead, knowing forward was still my only sane option. Turning sideways so the hedges were at my back and chest, I squeezed through, praying I wouldn't hit a wall.

The lead wolf snarled and I knew it was coming in for the kill. I put my head down and rushed into the thick brush, screaming.

And then I was free of the thicket and stumbling into an opening! I crashed to my knees, panting. I'd made it!

But rustling behind me told me I wasn't out of danger. Not by a long shot. If I could make it through the hedge, the wolves could as well.

The space around me was a large hedged circle. I

staggered to my feet and raced around the perimeter, searching for an escape. There had to be a way out! This couldn't be how it ended.

A loud snap sounded behind me and I whirled to see the head of a wolf emerge through the hedge.

My body shook like a leaf as the furry beast shook its massive body and turned its snout toward me. It snapped its jaws and licked the air, then slowly stalked my way. Another wolf emerged, then a third.

I held my breath and pressed myself deeper into the thick hedge, out of options. Terror ransacked my senses and I closed my eyes, awaiting the beasts' attacks. This was it. My intellect knew I wouldn't die, but my body wasn't listening to that part of my brain. My body was flooded with terror, and I prayed they would rescue me from the challenge, even though I'd go home a failure. Failure was better than suffering.

A heavy whack followed by whimpering cut through the night air.

I opened my eyes and saw a large figure standing between me and the wolves a mere ten paces away. The lead wolf laid motionless on his side as the other two approached the new threat with teeth bared. My heart jumped. I was being rescued!

The mysterious figure yanked something from his

cloak. I couldn't see what it was, but the wolves stopped cold, then slowly started backing away, growling. With a whimper, the two remaining beasts turned tail and hurried back to the hedge, then vanished through it.

I stood motionless as my savior turned and removed the hood of his cloak. It was the woodsman. He gripped a thick wooden club dripping in the wolf's blood. In his other hand, he held a small white crystal. A diamond. Again I heard Dean Kyra's words. *One will defend you.* This must have been what she meant.

The woodsman looked down at the diamond and then back to me.

I stood in stunned silence for a moment, unsure what to say.

"We need to move," he said, walking up to me. "They're scared off for now, but they may come back with others."

"How did you get here?" I asked. "Are you allowed to help me?"

"Asks the girl who almost got her head ripped off by three wolves," he said, "Of course I can help you. Didn't I just do it? I'm here to help those wise enough to accept my help. Come." He strode to the left side of the circular hedge and pulled away a heavy curtain of leaves. Behind was another narrow opening. A way out.

He motioned me over and I followed him into the thin passage, which he barely fit through, and out into another open space. He hurried across it to a rope ladder that had small wooden planks for steps.

"How did you know where to find me?" I asked.

"Not now. We need to get you out."

I stopped, an uneasy sense flittering in my chest. "I can't climb out. I have to go through."

He faced me, eyes narrowed. "Through? You're still playing their game? You've already lost! I need to get you back home before it's too late. You're on a clock, little girl. The sun is rising and your disappearance won't be taken lightly."

What was he talking about? He was confusing me. And I wasn't a little girl. But he was right about one thing: I was lost. I hadn't discovered my gift and I had no hidden stones. So maybe this was the only way? But something bothered me.

He noticed my hesitation and a scowl crossed his face.

"What are you waiting for?" he asked. "I thought you understood what was happening here."

"I just—"

"Don't give into their lies, Millie. They'll betray you every time! The only way out is with me. Trust me! I have never lied to you."

"I . . . I have to finish," I said. "I was chosen."

The woodsman studied me, his mouth twitching.

"Chosen? Who have you been talking to, Millie?" he asked.

I felt ashamed. He'd been so kind to me. I didn't want to disappoint him.

In a small, weak voice I answered, "The Great Teacher told—"

The woodsman started to chuckle, low and cruel. "The Great Teacher? The Great Teacher doesn't exist."

"I heard him." I felt a ball of embarrassment catch in my throat. "In the garden."

The woodsman glared. "Don't be a fool, little girl. The mind will play all kinds of tricks on you in this place. It's all part of their insane and terribly cruel game."

His words struck me hard. *You're just a foolish girl, Millie.* A ball of emotion in my throat grew and I bit my lip hard to keep tears of shame at bay. Had it really all been in my head? Had I tricked myself into thinking maybe I still belonged here, then thrown myself into the final challenge just to end up an even bigger fool?

You don't belong, Millie.

Something is wrong with you.

"There's still time for you to do what you know is best," the woodsman said. "You can put this childish fantasy behind you and be who you were meant to be."

"Because I don't belong here," I said.

"That's right. You belong somewhere safe, somewhere your inadequacies don't matter."

His words jarred me. "You think I'm inadequate?"

He took a deep breath and let it out slowly. "Don't you?"

Yes, I thought.

"You didn't complete either of the first two challenges. You don't have a gift or a stone, and if I hadn't shown up when I did, you'd be wolf chow," the woodsman said. "What makes you think *you* are chosen?"

I opened my mouth but nothing came. Tears slipped down over my lips as his words sank into my heart.

"I don't mean to hurt you," the woodsman said. He stepped away from the ladder, now wearing a kind face. "But I want you to see who you are so you won't do something stupid. If you'd listened to me, we wouldn't be here."

You're just a foolish, worthless girl.

Be better, Millie. Can you even be better?

"Now come," he said.

There was nothing else for me to do, so I went.

Millie.

I barely heard my name over the dense self-loathing that weighed on my heart like a stone, but it was there, soft and warm.

I am always with you.

I stopped. *The voice isn't real*, I told myself. It was only my mind playing tricks. I wouldn't fall for it again.

Remember the ways I love you.

I wanted to block the voice out, because it stirred a false hope that I was better than I thought I was. That was also just a trick. It had to be.

My love for you is bigger than the universe and longer than the life of a star.

I call you mine.

The Great Teacher's gentle voice started to sweep away some of my shame, drawing me in, filling me with a little peace. I was afraid to give in to it, because the woodsman had been right about so many things. What if he was right about me? But the voice of the Great Teacher was asking me to believe something else. I wasn't sure I could.

"What are you doing?" the woodsman snapped. "We're running out of time. Tick, tock, the sun is rising.

Time to get you home before it's too late."

Again with the sun rising, which made no sense to me. But in that moment I didn't care. I closed my eyes and let myself settle.

You are the one I chose, Millie Maven. The voice filled me with courage. *See yourself as I see you.*

"I hear him," I whispered. "He's with me now."

"You stupid, stupid little girl!" the woodsman hissed.

My eyes snapped wide and I caught my breath at the sight in front of me. The large-framed man I knew was gone and in his place stood a tall, thin figure. His black cloak hung from him as if he were only bones. His face was shadowed within the cloak's hood, and his skin was pale, pulled tightly across an angular face with deep-set eyes filled with hatred.

"I offer you everything," he snarled. "I offer you protection and comfort, and you want to betray me? For him?" He slid more than stepped toward me and I inched back, filled with terror. The man I'd trusted had become a monster.

"Don't you see, Millie Maven?" the man taunted. "I am the voice of reason that reminds you who you really are. I am the fear that protects and guides you. I am the voice of warning that keeps you safe from all threats. Without me, you are nothing!"

"Who are you?" I whispered.

"I have many names and many faces, but you can call me Soren." His eyes turned red as he spoke his name. "I have always been with you in different shapes and forms. Watching you, leading you. You can't reject me, you filthy, worthless girl! I won't let you."

He wrapped his fingers around my throat, lifting me off the ground. I struggled against his ironlike grip. The putrid smell of his breath filled my nostrils.

"You are mine," Soren growled. "It's time to remember who you really are." He tossed me and I landed hard on the ground. The wind left my lungs and stars dotted my vision. I rolled to my side and tried to push myself up, struggling to breathe.

"Let me remind you," Soren said.

His hand moved quickly and released a dark shadow, which streaked straight for me. The black form slammed into my chest and filled my heart. Pain pulsed throughout my entire body and I doubled over with a sharp cry.

Every dark thought I'd ever had about myself rushed over me like a tidal wave.

Worthless girl. Foolish girl. Weak and stupid.

You're dirty. Weak. There's something terribly wrong with you.

Nobody wants you. Nobody loves you.
You don't belong. You don't belong anywhere.

Over and over, the black fog smothered me with accusations until they were all I could hear. Until they were all I knew.

"Now you see who you really are," I heard Soren say.

Then the black fog was all I could see.

CHAPTER NINETEEN

Time seemed to stand still as I laid there lost in self-pity and condemnation. My eyes were swollen from crying and my whole body ached. A part of me hoped I would just fade into oblivion lying there on the cold ground.

Footsteps approached, and I thought Soren might be coming in for another round. *Let him,* I thought. *I have nothing left.*

A soft hand touched my shoulder and I flinched.

"It's okay," came a kind, familiar voice. "We're alone now."

I dared to open my eyes, and I saw bright eyes smiling down at me. A warm and loving face.

Rebecca.

"Are you real?" I croaked.

She brushed my cheek with her thumb. "As real as you are."

I swallowed deeply. "Is the Great Teacher real?"

She dipped her head like she was going to tell me a secret. "Would darkness be so threatened by something that wasn't?" She straightened and winked at me.

A sliver of hope slipped into my heart.

"You have a choice, Millie. You can listen to the voice of fear, which says you aren't enough and are in terrible danger. Or you can listen to the voice of truth, which says you are complete as you are and never in danger of being less. All your worries, insecurities, doubts, and fears come back to the one simple question: which voice will you listen to?"

"I failed the challenge," I objected.

"No, Millie. You're still in it, choosing your path. And you've done so well."

"I have?"

"Without a shred of doubt. I couldn't possibly be more proud of you."

Then she took my hand, unfolded my fingers, and placed something in my palm.

"A gift from the Great Teacher," she said. I didn't see what it was, but I could feel it round and cool against my skin.

"He chose you, sweetheart. Now finish what you

came to do. Remind them all who he is." She leaned down, kissed the top of my head, then hurried away.

She was proud of me?

I was still lost in the dark maze but something was different. A beating inside my chest was starting to grow. I felt warmth as if a fire was rising in my belly.

I call you mine. Perfect and whole. Washed clean in my death and life of all that blinds you to the truth. You are chosen.

Yes, I thought. *Yes, that's right.* I pushed myself up to my knees.

You're just a foolish, worthless girl.

The familiar voice of accusation tempted me once more and I cringed. Two voices said opposite things about me, and I could listen to only one. Could it be that simple? Could I simply turn toward the truth of the Great Teacher and be free from the shame that weighed me down like a ton of bricks?

Again, soft and powerful, the Great Teacher spoke over me. *You are beautiful as you are, and I call you mine.*

Kneeling there, head hung low, I whispered toward the ground, "I choose to listen to you."

Heat raced up my spine and through my arms.

"What did you say?" a voice rasped.

I jerked my head up and saw that Soren had

returned. The moment I saw him, my old mind whispered its lies.

Foolish, worthless, stupid girl! No one loves you. No one wants you.

My mind wanted to believe the words, because I always had. But it occurred to me that maybe Soren had gone because he was afraid of Rebecca.

My love for you is bigger than the universe and longer than the life of a star, the voice of peace whispered to me. *I call you mine, perfect and whole.*

His words filled me with courage. I pushed myself to my feet and turned to face Soren.

"I choose to listen to his truth," I said.

Fury twisted his face. "Stupid little girl," he spat.

"No," I said. My voice was weak, but I continued. "I'm not stupid." I took a step toward him. The light inside me grew, filling me with more courage.

"I am chosen," I said. "He called me to this."

Fear flashed across Soren's face. He opened his mouth to hurl insults, but I was tired of listening to him.

"He loves me and tells me I'm perfect and whole as I am." I took another step and my strength grew. "All you have ever done is lie to me."

The muscles in his jaw twitched. "Once you realize the truth, you'll come crawling back to me," he growled. "They always do."

"You're wrong."

"We'll see."

He raised his hand and his dark power rushed at me. I jerked up both my hands to protect myself, and the moment his dark fog stuck my palms, the scene filled with blinding light. The force of it knocked me off my feet. The brilliance lingered for a breath and then blinked out.

What had happened?

Then I remembered it, cool and in my palm: the gift from the Great Teacher. I glanced down and unclenched my fingers. There, shimmering in the moonlight, was a bronze medallion.

I looked up to see Soren staring at the bronze disk in my hand. He wore the expression of someone bitterly accepting defeat. There was a stump where his hand should have been, charred away to nothing. Smoke rose from his flesh as he shook in anger and pain.

"I tried to show you your true nature the easy way," he said through gritted teeth. "But you have made this more difficult than it needed to be. Now we will try the hard way. This isn't over, Millie Maven." Then he vanished—his body became smoke and floated away.

I stood, breathless but soaring with wonder and courage. I was still in the maze, and I was still alone.

No, that wasn't true.

You are never alone; I am always with you.

A warm breeze swept through the circular hedge. I closed my eyes and let the warmth cover me. Everything was different. It was as if I had been reborn right there in that maze. I had believed the truth and was made new.

When I opened my eyes, I saw the wind was blowing across the maze and through a new passage. I knew I was going to follow it.

And I knew wherever it led me was where I was born to go.

CHAPTER TWENTY

The wind led me around corners and down hidden paths, and I followed it without hesitation until I saw the grand maze's exit looming in the distance. I started to run. I was going to make it out! I burst from the maze and pulled up to a stop.

Kids were huddled in groups, whispering. The teachers were speaking in worried, hushed tones. I wondered what had happened. A boy named Reese saw me and shouted.

"She's here!"

They all turned to me, teachers and students alike, and shock and relief filled their faces. Then they were rushing toward me, all speaking at once.

"Millie!"

"Where were you?"

"Are you okay?"

Mac pushed through the crowd, rushed up to me, and wrapped me in a fierce hug. "I was so worried." She pushed back and then slugged my arm gently. "Don't do that to me!"

I rubbed the spot where she'd hit me and huffed. "What was that for?"

"I was scared to death! And when they couldn't find you—"

"What are you talking about?" I asked.

Dean Kyra parted the crowd, which fell silent.

"Millie," she said, "are you alright?"

"Yes, I'm fine."

She studied me for a long moment and finally dipped her head. "Where have you been? We've been looking for you for hours."

Hours? It hadn't been that long since I was separated from Mac and Boomer. I looked up and realized the sky was starting to lighten. Sunrise was coming. Was that what Soren had meant in talking about the sunrise? I sensed it was something else.

"Well?" Dean Kyra said, prompting me. "Where have you been for so many hours?"

They were all waiting to hear my explanation but I didn't have one. Time hadn't passed for me like it had for them. How was that possible?

"I don't know," I said. "I guess Soren did something."

Several teachers gasped. "What did you say?" Dean Kyra asked.

"Soren, in the maze he must have done something—"

"Enough." She lifted a hand and the desert setting vanished. We were once again in the meadow near the FIGS grounds.

Dean Kyra spoke to the teachers behind her. "Professor Alexandria, Professor Tomas, please escort Millie to my tent. The rest of you, back to camp. Rest. We will fetch you for the final medallion ceremony."

"Wait," Mac objected. "Can't I talk to her first?"

Boomer pushed himself to her side. "Yeah."

"Don't worry," Dean Kyra said. "We just want to make sure everything's alright. Then you can see her." She looked to Boomer. "Both of you."

Mac nodded, satisfied. Some students protested having to return to their tents, but they reluctantly followed Riggs toward the camp, leaving me alone with the teachers.

Professor Alexandria, the tall blond teacher with a constant stern expression, along with the short bald professor, Tomas, moved to my side. They escorted me to Dean Kyra's tent and directed me to sit. The dean took the seat across from me while the others gathered around. She didn't waste any time.

"I need you to tell me what happened to you in the maze, Millie." Her voice wasn't threatening or unkind, but there was no mistaking the urgency in her tone. "The truth, leaving nothing out."

I looked around at the teachers' concerned faces. After swallowing, I began at the beginning. I told them about with the flowers that attacked us, getting separated, the wolves, and the woodsman, who said his name was Soren. I told them about Rebecca and showed them the bronze medallion she'd given me. They listened without interrupting, wearing unreadable expressions.

When I finished, no one spoke. Dean Kyra leaned back in her chair. Professor Alexandria couldn't hold her tongue any longer and broke the silence.

"Blasphemy."

I looked at her, stunned. "That's what happened."

"You say the medallion was given to you by a woman named Rebecca?" Dean Kyra asked.

She spoke like she didn't know who Rebecca was.

"The gardener, yes."

I thought as the dean of the school she would know everyone who worked there. Or maybe she did know but was just surprised I had talked to Rebecca.

"She gave you the medallion?"

"Yes. She told me it was a gift from the Great Teacher," I answered.

"Why would the Great Teacher give her a medallion?" Professor Alexandria snapped. "This is lunacy."

"She does have a medallion in her hand," Professor Gabriel said. "Where else would it have come from? Soren?"

"Indeed!" Professor Claudia, the plump teacher, had a high-pitched voice. "Should we not be more concerned with Soren than the medallion?"

"And you say Soren's been speaking with you since you arrived here?" Professor Tomas asked.

"I thought he was my friend," I said, shrugging but also embarrassed.

"I agree with Alexandria," Professor Tomas said. "This seems very unlikely indeed."

"I'm not making it up," I said. "I promise."

"No one's accusing you of that," Dean Kyra said. "We're just trying to understand."

"Understand?" Professor Alexandria snapped. "She's also claiming to have spoken with the Great Teacher. Since when does a student speak to the Great Teacher? It requires proper channels, and ceremony. In all my years I've never heard directly from the Great Teacher! But he came to this child, who doesn't even have a gift or medallion to prove it?"

"On the contrary," Professor Gabriel interjected. "She does have a medallion. *His* medallion."

"Don't be ridiculous!" Professor Alexandria objected.

"His?" I asked.

Professor Claudia's eyes widened. "Could it be?"

"Could what be?" I asked.

"Where did you first meet the Great Teacher, Millie?" Professor Gabriel asked, eyes bright. His question startled me. He was the one who'd led me to the garden.

"In the FIGS garden," I said. "Under a huge willow tree."

I might as well have dropped a bomb in that place. They all stared at me, stunned except for Professor Gabriel, who only smiled and gave me a nod.

The others talked over each other.

"No one's seen the garden in a very long time," said one.

"Impossible!" objected another.

"How else would she know about it unless she's been there?"

"It must be true!"

"Nonsense!"

Dean Kyra held up her hand. "Enough!" They fell silent and she looked at me. "Will you give us one moment, Millie?"

I nodded and the teachers walked behind the curtain that divided the room. A moment later I heard their muffled voices, but I couldn't make out their words.

Swallowing nervously, I looked at the bronze medallion in my hand. It was like the rest, which transformed into their true color only when presented to a student at the medallion ceremony. I couldn't understand why it made some of the professors so upset. Wasn't the whole point for me to receive one of these?

The more I looked at it, the more mysterious the medallion became. It was heavy and light at the same time. Cool but tingling with heat. Professor Gabriel had said it was "his" medallion. The Great Teacher's. What did that mean?

I wanted to know, so I stood quietly and tip-toed closer to the curtain divider. They were all speaking in hushed tones, but I caught a couple phrases.

This is dangerous.

Delusions of speaking with the Great Teacher and the Father of Lies.

She cannot be trusted.

Removed from FarPointe Institute.

I withdrew. Fear crept into my chest; would they really send me back? How could they? I had completed the challenge and received a medallion.

"Psst."

Mac's head poked into Dean Kyra's tent. Boomer's popped up beside hers and I rushed over.

"What are you guys doing? You're not supposed to be here." But I couldn't stop myself from smiling. I was finally one of them.

"I know, but we had to make sure you're alright," Mac said.

"Yeah," Boomer agreed. "Are you okay?"

I glanced over my shoulder at the heavy curtain, then back at my friends. Excitement made my fingers tingle. "Look," I whispered, holding out my bronze medallion.

Mac squealed, then clamped her hand over her mouth. We stood quiet for a moment, checking to make sure we hadn't drawn any unwanted attention. Mac lowered her hand.

"You got a medallion!"

"Yeah, in the maze," I said.

"I didn't think it worked like that," Boomer said.

"I don't think it's supposed too," I answered. "But it did for me, and I don't know why."

"Tell us everything," Mac said.

As quickly as my mouth would work, I spun through the details. My heart raced as I relived my confrontation with Soren like it was happening to me all over again.

"How terrifying!" Mac said when I'd finished. "Who is Soren? Why hasn't anyone else seen him?"

"I don't know," I said. "But I don't think I was supposed to see him."

"Your medallion's still bronze. What's your gift?" Boomer asked. "That will help us know what color it's going to become during the ceremony."

I paused, feeling self-conscious. "I don't know. Maybe something will happen at the ceremony."

"It must be something pretty amazing," Mac said. "I always knew you were special, Millie Maven."

We held one another's eyes for a moment, and my heart felt like it might burst.

"What happens if Soren comes back?" Boomer asked. He looked afraid and I didn't blame him.

"I don't know," I said. "I don't even know if I'm going to get to stay."

"They have to let you stay," Mac said.

"Yeah," Boomer said. "If you go, we go."

Someone cleared their throat and we all turned to see Dean Kyra standing there, her face amused. "Is that so, Mr. Talley?"

Boomer froze and mumbled something that made no sense.

"You can't send her home," Mac said. "Please, Dean

Kyra. She deserves to be here."

"I'll catalog your concern, Miss Spitzer. For now I will ask you to return to your tents and rest up for the final medallion ceremony," Dean Kyra said. "All will become clear then."

Mac and Boomer nodded, then turned to leave me alone with the dean.

"You have good friends," she said. "That's important."

It seemed the other teachers had gone, and I was glad I didn't have to interact with Professor Alexandria.

"You'll have to forgive us," Dean Kyra said. "I imagine all of this feels very troubling."

I call you mine. Chosen. His warmth filled my chest and I smiled.

"It's okay. Actually, I feel more okay than I have in a long time."

"How so?" she asked.

"Honestly, yesterday I was planning to leave. I was sure I didn't belong here and that I wasn't worthy of a medallion. I don't remember my life before FIGS, but I don't think it was good. And I'm pretty sure everything I've ever believed about myself is a lie. I've never felt good enough, but I'm starting to now."

Dean Kyra hung onto my every word.

"Because he told me I was," I said, feeling his love

touch my heart. "The Great Teacher said he chose me for this. And then Rebecca gave me this medallion."

"The woman in the garden."

"You really don't know her? I tried to go back to the garden, but it was gone. I really was there though."

"I know, child. As for Rebecca, it seems she was sent to you from the Great Teacher. To watch over you."

Like an angel, I thought, but my mind was moving to other questions.

"What about Soren? Why me? What does he want?"

"All will become clear in the weeks to come. For now, all you must know is that all things work together for good."

Dean Kyra studied me and I wished I could hear what she was thinking.

"I'll admit, I don't know what your medallion means for you or for us," she said. "The uncertainty does make me a little uncomfortable."

She paused before continuing.

"Still, I've always believed in this process. We don't give our students gifts or medallions. They come to those who are meant to have them. I don't see why this is any different."

"But I don't have a gift," I said.

"Yes, that is new. But you do have a medallion, so let

us see what happens at the ceremony."

She believes me, I thought. *And she's going to let me stay.*

"I think it's best for everyone that you stay here, where we can continue to see what comes of this unusual turn of events. I want to be apprised of everything: if you start to develop strengths, if you continue to interact with the Great Teacher, if you see Soren. I won't be able to help or protect you if I don't know what's going on. Do you understand?"

"Yes."

She smiled. "Good. Why don't you rest here for a little while? I'll wake you before the ceremony."

At the mention of sleep, I felt exhausted. How long had it been since I'd slept? I couldn't remember.

"I'm filthy," I said, looking at my torn and dirtied uniform.

"Never mind that. Sleep."

I nodded, and she pointed to a lush couch that seemed to be calling my name. I collapsed into the soft cushions, holding my medallion close to my heart.

Within moments, I was fast asleep.

CHAPTER TWENTY-ONE

I'd slept for over three hours when Dean Kyra woke me and instructed me to freshen up for the ceremony. After a quick change of clothes and a splash of water on my face, I hurried out to see that many of the students were already waiting under the canopy at the head of the camp.

My arrival stirred whispers from the other kids. Surely everyone knew I'd received a medallion in a very unconventional way. All watched me closely. It wasn't just them, though. The whole camp seemed full of anticipation.

"Welcome to the final medallion ceremony," Dean Kyra said. "Let us begin."

The other four students who'd gone into the maze without gifts all succeeded. Dean Kyra called their names one by one, presenting them with medallions that changed color. I held mine at my chest. My heart raced as possibilities skipped through my mind.

"Millie Maven," Dean Kyra finally called out.

I tried to still the tremble in my hands as I walked up and stood before the beautiful headmistress. She was an ally, I knew. As I looked up at her, I felt some of my nerves dissolve. I saw Professor Alexandria watching with skepticism.

"This is a new one for me," Dean Kyra said, loud enough for everyone to hear. "I am not presenting you with a medallion, because it was given to you by a power beyond me."

Students whispered as she held out her hand and I placed my fist in her palm. My medallion was tucked inside my clenched fingers.

She smiled. "I usually announce a gift at this time, but your gift is yet to be known. What I do know is that the source of our power has reached out to you in a way that hasn't been seen in my lifetime. This medallion you hold comes from the Great Teacher himself."

Her words stirred more whispers.

Dean Kyra spoke over the mild disruption. "You also encountered the Father of Lies, Soren, who defies the Great Teacher with his very being. But you, Miss Maven, are still standing, so whatever power your gift produces must be great. Few have lived to tell stories such as yours."

She leaned down and lowered her voice. "Let's see what is to come." She looked at my hand. "Please open your hand, my child."

I slowly opened my fingers to reveal the bronze medallion. But it wasn't bronze anymore. It was a brilliant red, the color of blood.

Dean Kyra stared in amazement. "So, it is true."

"Impossible." Professor Alexandria looked pale and perplexed.

"What is it?" Mac called, speaking for all those waiting. "What color is it?"

Dean Kyra held up my arm so all could see the crimson medallion dangling from my fingers.

"The color of the Great Teacher," Dean Kyra said. "A red medallion, the first to ever be presented to a student since the time the Great Teacher himself walked these halls in the flesh."

The students' whispers broke into loud rumblings.

"What does it mean?" Riggs asked.

"Wait, the Great Teacher is real?" Chaplin said.

Students started shouting.

"How did she get it?"

"What does it do?"

"I always knew she would get a medallion."

Then above them all, resounding and whiny: "She doesn't even have a gift," Doris spat. "She shouldn't get to stay."

I tuned the voices out and stared at the bright-red medallion in my palm. A red medallion, the color of the Great Teacher, a medallion that hadn't been seen since he was here. On the surface, like many I had seen, an image was itched into the medal. A circle, I thought, formed of twigs, leaves, and some thorns.

"A crown," Dean Kyra whispered as the madness ensued. "His."

Of course. It made perfect sense. I smiled, feeling the power of his love wash through me.

"Can you feel him now?" Dean Kyra asked.

I looked up and nodded.

She leaned forward and spoke under her breath for only me to hear. "People will try to convince you that you aren't worthy of that red medallion, and it will feel like they are right at times. Please try not to listen to their lies." She gave me a broad smile. "I have always believed in you."

My chest filled with such joy that I thought it might burst. A warm breeze swept over my shoulders, and with it, the voice of love.

I call you mine. You are chosen, Millie Maven.

Dean Kyra held her hands up and quickly drew everyone to order.

"There is much we do not know," she said. "But if this medallion has been given, then it was meant for this time. And it was meant for you, Miss Maven. May you discover this medallion's power and align to it in fullness. May your intentions be good. May your heart be strong."

She smiled wide at me, and I felt I might cry from sheer joy.

"Welcome to FarPointe Institute, Miss Maven." Dean Kyra raised her eyes to the rest of the students. "Welcome, all of you. Tomorrow, you will move into the campus and begin your training. I sense only great things to come, but for now we celebrate!"

The teachers and Leads started clapping and cheering for us as I rejoined the group of students who were also applauding. Many jumped up and down, excited. Some embraced. A few even cried. Most rushed me like water, and for the next hour I told the story over and over of how I received my medallion.

In time I was interrupted by delightful music played by Professor Gabriel, who had a fiddle perched on his shoulder. The tune was a joyful jig, and he was soon joined by Professor Tomas who kept beat with two bongos on the ground.

The other professors started singing a song they all knew. The Leads joined in, and soon everyone was singing, even grumpy Professor Alexandria. Dancing ensured that the laughter continued. The entire world felt perfect, captured by joy that couldn't be disturbed.

I danced with Mac as Boomer shuffled along beside us. We laughed until our sides hurt, stuffed our faces with a feast of turkey and pork that had appeared during the festivities, and devoured enough cookies for a year. Even Dash and Doris seemed to enjoy themselves, despite the dark glances Doris threw my way. The party lasted all afternoon and until the sun set.

As the festivities finally wound down, I collapsed onto the grass beside my tent, sweaty and exhausted. Mac dropped beside me and Boomer quickly joined. We laid on our backs and stared up at the sky as the stars started to appear, pondering what was in store for us.

"I'll never eat another cookie again," Boomer said, holding his belly. He let out a groan.

Mac and I laughed.

Mac titled her head so that it touched my shoulder. She sighed. "I hope we never have to leave this place."

Her words reminded me of what Soren had said. I had until sunrise to get back. But Soren was a liar. He meant nothing to me now.

"Me too," I said.

Crickets started to play their nighttime song as the warm breeze swept across our tired but exhilarated bodies. And with it his voice filled my mind and soul.

I call you perfect, whole, and loved.

I chose you to see my love in you so that you can show them all.

"I will," I whispered.

Boomer groaned again and Mac couldn't keep from laughing. It infected me and then even Boomer, until we were all caught up in delirious laughter. I didn't know what was coming, but in that moment, I knew who I was.

I was the girl with the red medallion.

Chosen by the Great Teacher.

And that was enough.

TO BE CONTINUED

CONTINUE THE QUEST IN BOOK 2